What Remains

Marionette Zombie Series
Book 13

SB Poe

ISBN: 9798507100804

WHAT REMAINS

	Acknowledgments	i
1	Part 1 What Was	
	The Light Show	4
2	Daybreak	36
3	For Safekeeping	51
4	The Other End of the Road	70
5	Red Flag	89
6	Where it all Began	100
	Part 2 What Remains	
7	Keys and Locks	119
8	For Now	132
9	Moving	147
10	The Hour Grows Late	164

ACKNOWLEDGMENTS

Thank you all for coming on this journey with me.

What Remains

Part 1

What Was

The Light Show

"Roll the window up, it's chilly." Theresa said.

"Don't you think we've gone far enough?" Abby asked.

"I want to make sure we get a clear view." Joel said, as he leaned forward to look through the windshield. The radio was broadcasting the news on the hour.

"In other news, the world welcomed the birth of the seventh great-grandchild of the Queen of England today. The palace announced the birth

of Victoria Lennox Winfield this morning. The Queen was said to be extremely pleased and mother and baby are doing very well. Sadly, the same can't be said for the sudden outbreak of the recently discovered Marionette virus that began plaguing the island of Madagascar a few days ago. Local government officials are continuing to call for international intervention in what is rapidly growing into a humanitarian crisis, as hospitals appear to be overwhelmed and there are now sporadic reports that it has spread to the African continent. Officials at the National Institute of Health said they are aware but not overly concerned but did take the opportunity to remind all Americans to get their annual flu shot. And finally astronomers at the Willis Observatory at UGA say that tonight's brief meteor shower from the passing of the Morsumbra Comet will be most visible in areas with limited light pollution but will wane over the next few days. Next news at ten."

"See? It's going to be much better out here." Joel

said. The car's headlights lit the field ahead as it eased around the winding country road.

"Look!" Abby leaned forward and pointed. "All those eyes look spooky."

"Deer." Joel said. "Lots of them."

"Abigail Patterson put your seatbelt on." Theresa snapped.

"Sorry." She leaned back and buckled the belt.

"Next place I can find to pull off the road, we'll stop. We're going to get a great view out here." Joel eased his foot off the accelerator slightly. The road widened in front of an old country store that the kudzu had mostly reclaimed. The car stopped. They all got out.

"It's creepy." Abby said.

"Everything's creepy to you." Joel said.

"Yeah, well out in here in the middle of nowhere standing in front of this place is kind of creepy." Theresa said. "You gotta admit."

“You know my mother grew up just down the road from here, right?” Joel said.

“And she moved to the city as quick as she could. She told me.” Theresa said.

“Look back that way.” Joel pointed. The glow of Atlanta was distinct. The halo of light against the black outline of the distant trees made where they stood that much darker. An ancient bare oak broke the sky into puzzle pieces ahead of the horizon. “Don’t you ever want to get away from all that?”

“This won’t be another one of those ‘I think we should just move to the country and raise goats’ trips, will it?” Theresa smiled as she came around the side of the car.

“No Dad. Please tell me you’re not going to start that again.” Abby chimed in.

“All I’m saying is that it would be nice to live a little simpler, even if it’s just for a while. Get in touch with nature.”
“Why?” Abby asked.

"Just to see if we can. Proof of concept. You never know if you don't try."

"Then I'll guess I'll never know because there is no way you're ever going to talk me into buying a farm and raising goats." Theresa said.

"What is it with you and goats? I think you secretly want to raise goats. I've seen your phone. All those baby goat videos in your favorites."

"There's a bunch of recipe videos in my favorites too but that doesn't mean I plan on cooking them. The Apron Store delivers all we need." Theresa laughed as she elbowed him in the side.

"One can dream, can't he?" Joel said.

"It's starting." Abby said, as she pointed to the darkened sky.

A few streaks flashed above their heads. At first it was sporadic, one here, another there. The first long streak occurred fifteen minutes after Abby had lifted her hand to the sky. Fifteen minutes after that, the ground around them grew brighter as the darkness above filled with short streaks and long running tails of light across the sky. Joel glanced at his wife and child and could see the reflection of the sky in their eyes. All of them had smiles on their faces as the light show held them entranced for another half hour. The sky slowly returned to a slightly darker shade than before as the night passed by. The glow of the city once again took over the western sky.

“We’d have never seen all that from there.” Joel nodded towards the west.

“That was amazing.” Abby said.

“You do have your moments.” Theresa said.

As they began the long drive home, she reached over and squeezed his hand. An hour later, they pulled into their driveway. The carport light was out. Joel glanced down the street. Two street lamps down the road were out. The next neighbor was half a mile away since the Taylor’s moved from the house across the road. The zoning laws around the creek had left five houses with almost full acre lots, while the rest of the surrounding neighborhoods were slightly under a quarter of that size. The Taylor's had sold Joel the house he had now when they built the one across the road. That had been a few years ago, but the Taylor's only child had now moved several states away. They decided it was time to move to the beach, so they did. Even though it had been almost a month since it had sold, the new family was still out in Nevada. The man who bought it, Mr. Long, had knocked on Joel's door the day they closed. He had introduced himself and told Joel it would probably be another few months before they closed their affairs and moved in. The way he had said 'close our affairs' immediately made Joel think he was some kind of mafia stool pigeon in witness protection. He had left his business card, an insurance salesman, definitely Mafioso Joel thought, and asked Joel to call him if there was some issue with the house. Since then, the house had sat empty and undisturbed. And dark.

"I think the power's out." Joel said. The carport

light flickered on. "Magic." He smiled.

They walked into the house. It was still warm, so the power had not been out long. Theresa walked to the refrigerator and opened the door. Everything was still cool to the touch.

"Guess it was just a blip." She said.

"I'm going to bed." Abby announced as she headed towards the back of the house.

"No phone. No texting." Theresa called.

"No promises." Abby called back.

"Abby!" Theresa raised her voice.

"She's fifteen." Joel said. "You remember fifteen?"

"I didn't have a cell phone." She said.

"And if you had?" He asked.

"I'd probably be just like she is." Theresa conceded.

"Don't hate the player." He said.

"You're a dork." She smiled.

"Not just any dork, your dork." He said. "Forevah."

"Unfortunately." She smiled as she punched his arm.

They went down the same hallway Abby had just gone down and past her room. The master was the last one on the right. He glanced into the spare bedroom as they made their way down the hall. The three-bedroom ranch had been home for just over a two years and he still hadn't unpacked everything. They had sold their house in Conley and moved north of downtown, so Theresa, who worked as a guidance counselor at Brenthold Elementary, could be closer to her job. Joel was a staff writer for a hunting and fishing magazine focusing on the positive environmental effects of the hunting community. His work mostly consisted of talking to a lot of biologists and other scientists about species adaptations and how proper management of herd populations can protect entire subordinate species from disease and starvation. The best days were the few he actually spent in the field with hunters who work hard at keeping their game in good shape because they know better than any spreadsheet could ever tell you that if you have a healthy and thriving deer and turkey population most everything else is in balance. It doesn't happen otherwise. Most of his days are spent in a small office just off Peachtree where he has to commute at least three days a week. Tomorrow isn't one of those days, so they took the opportunity to take a ride out and see the meteor shower. He was glad they had.

He reached over to the nightstand and grabbed the remote. She came out of the bathroom as he turned the television on.

"Did you check on her?" She asked.

"She's watching some movie about a dance competition and I think, vampires. Don't quote me on that though." He said as he flipped the channel guide, glancing over his reading glasses to the screen to see the words and back behind his reading glasses to see the numbers on the remote.

“Did you tell her to shut it off and go to bed?” She asked.

“Uh, yeah, sure.” He lied.

“Wow, you really look old.” She smirked. He glanced at her over his glasses.

“How long now? Two months until the big day?” She asked.

“I don’t know what you’re talking about.” He said as he glanced back down.

“Sure you do. The big five oh. Fifty. The halfway home day.” She smiled.

“The average lifespan of a man is around seventy-five years so technically the halfway point was a decade or so ago but hey, thanks for the encouragement.” He said without looking up.

“What’s the average lifespan for a woman?” She asked as she pulled the sheet back and slid into the bed.

"A little longer. Seventy-eight or so." He said. He could see her doing the quick calculation in her head.

"You've passed it too, honey. Several years ago."

"Barely." She said.

"Of course. How foolish of me. I forgot you were a child bride." He laughed.

He hit select and the channel changed to the news. What he expected to see was a talking head recapping all the day's events in the stock market. He didn't care about the market, but the man's monotonous British accent always helped him fall asleep. The voice was gone. A somewhat frantic sounding foreign language under a slightly less frantic sounding English translation replaced it.

"The horrible outbreak of this newly discovered Marionette rabies virus that has been ravaging the island nation of Madagascar has now crossed into Europe. Spanish authorities are reporting Marionette outbreaks in the port town of Barbate

and in Vigo on the Portuguese border. There are images being broadcast from the Spanish authorities of local security cameras that have captured some of the impact of these outbreaks. We want to warn you that some of these images are quite disturbing and we also want to reiterate that these images have not been independently authenticated."

The screen flipped over to a traffic camera positioned near an intersection. The fisheye lens distorted some of the edges, but the traffic was stopped and most of the cars had their doors open. Between the vehicles, there were shapes that came into focus as the image began to make sense in their heads. Making sense was probably not the right way to put it. Realizing what they were witnessing, understanding the images were not part of some horror movie and feeling the veneer of safety being ripped away would be some of the ways to put it. Making sense was not what the images did. He felt her sit up in the bed.

"Joel?" She asked. "It that real? Is that really happening?"

"My god." He said.

His phone vibrated on the nightstand. Hers did too. They both grabbed them. The Emergency Action message that usually alerted them to a nearby tornado or thunderstorm was flashing a civil defense emblem.

"Local emergency, please shelter in place."

The sound of sirens began erupting in the distance outside the bedroom window as his feet hit the floor. She brushed by him and rushed down the hallway. She returned moments later with Abby in tow.

"Sit here." She pointed to the bed.

"What did I do? Have you been going through my phone or something? Why am I in trouble?" She asked.

"You're not in trouble." He said as he pulled a

sweatshirt on.

“Should I go through your phone?” Theresa asked.

“Not now, honey.” He said.

A loud squeal of tires under heavy braking sounded outside the bedroom window, followed by a louder sound of crumpling metal and breaking glass. The sky outside the window flashed violently as the transformer exploded. Everything went dark. They all jumped up. Joel and Theresa made their way down the hallway, with Abby close behind. He threw the front door open. The headlights of the car pointed in two directions and reflected off the trees back onto the road. The power pole swung from the lines. Its tether to the earth shattered when the car plowed into it, breaking it clean in half. The car that hit it was almost destroyed. The front was crumpled up against the driver, who hung lifeless in the seatbelt with the jagged, splintered end of the pole shoved where the head should have been. Blood covered everything. Joel turned and grabbed Abby’s shoulders as she came up behind.

"Stop. Don't look. Stay right here. Better yet, go back into our room and stay there." He said.

"But Dad..." Abby started.

"Now. Right now." He said.

She turned and disappeared down the hall. Theresa held her hand to her mouth as she processed the scene in front of her. She could see the hole in the windshield on the passenger side and her eyes unconsciously followed the arc the thing that made the hole would have taken. Her eyes widened when she saw the small dark shape in the street. She saw the foot twitch and it broke the spell. She started forward. He grabbed her arm.

"Where are you going?" He said.

"Oh my god, Joel, it's a child." She pointed at the shape in the street. "Call 911." She started forward again. Joel reached his hand down and realized his phone was still in the bedroom. He turned.

"I'll be right back. Be careful." He called, but she was already halfway across the yard. He went back to his room and grabbed his phone, pausing long enough to grab the flashlight from the nightstand drawer. Abby sat on the edge of the bed.

"What's going on?" She asked.

"I don't know yet. Stay here." He turned and headed back towards the door.

She paused at the edge of the road and looked again. The body was still. Then she saw a small twitch.

"Stay still. Help is coming." She said as she closed the distance between her and the child. She knelt down. The child slowly lifted one of its hands off the asphalt; she grabbed it and held it.

"It's okay. It's gonna be okay. Shh." She could see the terribly twisted legs folded across one another in jeans that were shredded and soaked with blood. The hand felt frighteningly cold. She instinctively rubbed and patted it. "It's okay. Help is on the way." She turned her head to see if Joel was coming. She felt a sharp pain in her arm and the weight of the child pulling her hand down. She spun her head around and jerked her arm free. The scream from her lips barely registered, and she was almost ashamed. Surely the child didn't bite her. Surely that couldn't have happened.

The child tried to push itself up on its elbows. She felt the blood running down the back of her arm. It made no sense. But it was real. Her mind filled with the images from the television. She heard her own voice ask, 'is that real?' in her head. Her eyes grew wide. She scrambled back, scrapping her knee on the asphalt as she tried to gain her feet. Joel crossed the yard at a sprint as she tried to stand. He met her as she stumbled a few more feet from the child. She almost collapsed in his arms, but he braced her and held her up.

"What?" He asked. "What happened?" He pulled his hand back. It was wet with blood. "Oh my god, what happened to you?"

"He bit me. The kid bit me." She turned back towards the thing in the road. "Like what we saw on the television."

"You don't think that..." Joel started.

"I don't know what to think but he bit me."

Joel trained the beam of the flashlight on the child. Its eyes reflected in the light. Pale. They could see the gash along the side of its head. Blood covered its whole right shoulder and part of the collarbone stuck straight up. It moved its arm and the collarbone moved with it. It braced its hand on the ground and pushed itself up. The bones stuck further out.

"Oh, my god." Theresa said. She backed away, pulling Joel with her. "Something's bad wrong Joel. We need to get inside."

"Yeah, yeah. Let's go." They turned and started back across the yard. Joel looked back as they got to the door. The child was still trying to sit up. He closed the door behind them and locked it. He dialed 911 again. The line never connected.

Joel walked out of the kitchen carrying three battery-powered lanterns he had dug out the boxes still stacked in the spare bedroom. He had a bottle of coke and box of crackers under his arm. Abby was sitting on the floor in her room, turning the crank on the emergency radio, trying to find some music. He wasn't sure the thing still worked. It had been stuffed in the box of camping gear with all the other things he hadn't unpacked yet. The small flashlight on the top of it had power though, so maybe there was hope.

He sat the lanterns down on the nightstand. Theresa was sitting up in the bed.

"How you feeling?" He asked.

"It's sore. It feels like it's swelling." She said.

He reached over and wrapped his hand around her forearm. The bite was just above her elbow on the back of her arm. He gently rotated her arm a little. She winced.

“Sorry.” He said.

It didn’t feel warm. It felt cold. He held the lantern up. He could see darker blue veins in the light. Maybe it was the LED bulb. He touched her skin. His hand against her skin made it look even worse. His skin was pink, hers was pale around the bandage he had put over it after they washed the wound with peroxide. And his skin didn’t have little blue veins.

“It seems okay.” He lied. “Here.” He handed her the bottle of coke and reached into his shirt pocket to withdraw the two pills she sent him after. She swallowed them down.

“That was from the trip to the dentist when you had that abscess, right?” She asked.

“Yep.”

“Good.” She took a cracker and slowly chewed. She wasn’t sure if her stomach was upset from the bite or from what she had seen, but she hoped a coke and a cracker would cure either. She glanced towards the hallway.

"Have you looked outside?" She whispered to Joel.

"It's still in the road."

"God Joel, what is happening?" She asked.

"I don't know."

'This is an announcement from the emergency broadcast system. Please stay tuned to this station for the latest FEMA Emergency report. This is an announcement from the emergency broadcast system. Please stay tuned to this station...'

"Dad?" Abby came into their room carrying the radio.

"Good job." He said.

She dropped onto the edge of the bed. She sat the radio down between them.

'Due to an unexpected and ongoing

outbreak of the Marionette virus, local authorities in the city of Atlanta and the surrounding counties have declared an imminent threat emergency. All interstate travel through Atlanta is now closed. A shelter in place order is in effect. A curfew is in effect until further notice. Do not leave your homes unless absolutely necessary to save life and limb. Should evacuations become necessary, there will be further instructions on this channel. Make preparations now in the event conditions warrant evacuations. Gather at least two days' food and water for each person in the household if possible. We will provide further information on the Marionette virus as it becomes available. To repeat, due to an unexpected and ongoing outbreak of the Marionette virus local...'

"Curfew? Shelter in place?" Abby asked. "What does that mean?"

"It means we stay right here until it's safe." Theresa said.

"Safe from what?" She asked.

"Whatever's going on." Theresa said.

"How are we supposed to gather food and water if we can't leave our house? These people make no sense." Abby said flippantly.

Joel glanced at his wife.

"They're doing the best they can honey." Theresa said. She looked at Joel. They both turned.

Joel could see lights through the bedroom window. He stood and walked down the hallway. A car had pulled up to the wreckage in the road. The lights shone across the road and towards his house and he could see the silhouette of the body on the ground. The car backed up and turned around. He heard the chirp of tires as it rapidly retreated. The world outside went dark again. He walked back to the bedroom.

"Everything okay?" Theresa asked.

"Yeah, someone was trying to get somewhere. They turned around." He said.

“Can I use the bathroom?” Abby asked.

“Can you?” Joel smirked.

“I mean with the power out and all.” She stood.

“Yes, honey, ignore him, he’s a dork. Here.” She handed her the lantern by the bed. Joel grabbed the other one and turned it on. “Keep it with you.”

She walked down the hallway and into the bathroom. The hall went dark again as she closed the door. Joel grabbed the radio and hit scan. It landed at another station.

‘And you saw this?’ A reporter’s voice came through the speaker. ‘Yeah, it was right down the street. They were eating her.’ Joel hit scan again. *‘The National Institute of Health spokesman was rather vague just now but to recap that extraordinary press conference is our own medical expert Dr. Chase Herzog. Doctor?’ ‘It is obvious to me that the NIH doesn’t know what it is dealing with. And in their defense I don’t think any of us do. A few things are becoming more*

apparent though.' 'What is that, Doctor?' 'One is that this is most likely a virus that is spread by direct contact, scratches, bites, etc. and two that we have no treatment. I would add the most concerning aspect in the limited information we have is that it appears to be astronomically lethal.' 'What should we do, doctor?' 'Honestly? Pray.' 'Pray? Shouldn't we do a little more than that?' 'There is nothing we can do. There is nothing else to do.' 'So you think the NIH is hiding the worst....' 'What the hell does it matter what they are doing? Don't you understand? Can't you see outside your own fucking window.....' The radio went silent briefly. 'We apologize to the listening audience for that unintended outburst.' A song from 1984 began playing.

Joel hit scan again and it landed on the repeating emergency broadcast, chiding listeners to forever stay tuned. He turned the volume down and looked into her eyes. They were wet with tears.

"It's going to be okay." He said.

"No, it's not." She wiped her eyes. "It's not. I can feel whatever it is inside me now. My shoulder is completely numb. I can't feel it at all."

"What do you want me to do?" He looked at his phone. The cellular icon was gone. It was now an expensive brick. "I'm going to take you to a hospital." He stood. She grabbed his hand.

"No. You are not going to take me anywhere." She said. "It's too dangerous out there. You heard the radio. The roads are closed."

"It's not too dangerous. You're hurt. We can make it."

"I'm hurt. But she isn't." Theresa nodded towards the hall. "We don't know what's going to happen to me but it's going to happen. There's nothing we can do to stop it. It's already happening. I screwed up and I'm going to pay for that. But you can't make her pay for it too. You can't pay for it either. And she's going to need you. You're going to need her."

"I'm not going to just do nothing." Joel said.

"Wait until morning." She said.

"It is morning."

"Wait until the sun is up. Just a few hours. I'll be fine."

"And if you get worse?"

"Wait. Please."

"Why? Why are you doing this?" Joel asked. He sat down beside her.

"I'm scared." She said.

"Me too."

"I'm scared for you."

"For me?"

"You heard the doctor on the radio. Astronomically lethal. That's what he said." She said. "And no treatment. So I can't be scared for me anymore. There's no point. There's nothing they can do. Maybe I'll be lucky, but maybe not. But you, I am scared for you. If it happens, if I... you're going to have to pull her through this all by yourself. I don't know if I could do that if it were you lying here."

"It should be me lying there." Joel said. "Please let me take you..."

"No. In the morning."

"Why?"

"It has to be safer for her now. You can't take chances. Not unless you have to. We can wait until the sun is up. It will be safer. Maybe not much, but still safer than going out in the dark. And that's what you have to do now. Make it safer for her. Promise me you won't put her in danger. Promise me you'll keep her safe." She said.

"I'm focusing on you now. We have to..." Joel started.

"Shut up. Just shut up and listen to me. Really listen to me. Don't try to do the right thing. Don't do what you think you should do. I'm going to tell you what you have to do. And you have to do everything you can to do it. You have to keep her safe. There is nothing else now. No matter what happens to me. No matter what happens to anyone else. You have to keep her safe. We worked so hard to get her here. You have to do it. She can't do it herself. She thinks she can. She thinks she's grown but she's not. Hell, I don't think I was until right now. But now I know, I know all that matters, all that ever really mattered, was her. It doesn't matter if it's today or tomorrow or twenty years from now, when I'm gone, when you're gone, she's all that will be left of us. She's the best thing we've ever done and she has to keep going. You have to make sure of it. Even if you have to let me go. You have to promise me."

He looked at her. The lantern cast a dull white light around the room. Her skin was ashen. Gray. Her eyes were sunken. He could see the faint traces of the blue veins creeping further down her arm as he held her hand in his. Her palm felt cold.

The realization slowly crept over him. His mind began to slow down. Anger at his powerlessness began to build in his stomach. Black pitch wanted to burst forth from his veins to rage against how truly helpless he was and how inadequately he protected her. But her words came through. Abby. Everything he had failed at tonight, he could make right. He began to feel some resolve. But the moment of courage he felt faltered when he looked into her eyes again.

“I don’t know how. Not without you.” He said.

“Yes, you do. You have to. And I need to know you will. Promise me.” Theresa said.

“I promise I will do everything I can to keep her safe.” Joel said. “But I failed so bad already, I couldn’t keep you safe.”

“You didn’t fail. You won’t fail. Things just happened. This wasn’t your fault. It wasn’t anyone’s fault. We didn’t know. That’s not failing. That’s just life.” She said.

He sat holding her hand as she slipped off to sleep. He met Abby in the hallway and they both went to the living room to wait for the sun to rise.

Daybreak

He leaned against the doorframe. He couldn't hear what they were saying, but he could see Theresa struggling to raise her hand to brush Abby's hair out of her eyes. The tears slowly slid down his face. He turned away as he wiped his cheek with the back of his hand. As he walked down the hallway, he glanced at the window in the living room. He sat down on the couch and could see the light rising in the eastern sky. He wanted them to have these few minutes alone.

Abby reached up and took her mother's hand as she stroked her hair.

"You know how proud I am of you, right? You are

exactly what I always dreamed about." She smiled through the tears in her eyes.

"Mom, I don't understand. Why won't you let us take you to the doctor? Please?" Abby pleaded.

"Not yet. Wait just a little while. Just sit here with me right now. When we go to the hospital, this might be the last chance I get to be like this with you." She said.

"Stop saying that. Why are you saying that?" Abby asked.

"I want you to be strong. I can't pretend...I can't..." She coughed. Her eyes widened. She coughed again. "I love..." She coughed one more time.

Joel heard her coughing and ran back down the hallway. He paused at the door.

"Mom? Mom? Mom, can you hear me? MOM?" Abby leaned forward.

"Abby?" Joel said.

Abby turned and faced him. Her face was

streaked with tears.

"She's not breathing."

"Honey?" He came around the bed. "Theresa?" He moved faster. "HONEY CAN YOU HEAR ME?" He turned to Abby. "Move." She stood. He threw the blanket back and scooped Theresa up in his arms. She was almost too light.

He brought her to the end of the bed and laid her down on the floor. His mind flashed to a beautiful summer day. He wasn't sure why he was there, scouts? summer camp?, he didn't know. But he remembered the lesson. CPR. He looked down at his wife. She looked gone. He found the spot on her chest and pressed. The lesson came to his mind. One, two, three,... all the way to twenty. He tilted her head back and breathed two breaths into her mouth. He started counting again.

"Please Theresa, please. Not now. Not now." He pressed to thirty and gave her two breaths. He paused and listened. She didn't move. He started again.

"Please God, please." He could hear Abby crying in the corner. He blocked it out. He pressed harder. He felt the rib crack under his hand. He paused and looked at her. She didn't move. He gave her two breaths and started pushing again.

"PLEASE HELP ME. PLEASE SOMEONE HELP ME!!!!!" He screamed at the sky.

The sweat ran down his face. He looked at her again. He gave her one more breath. She didn't move. He touched his lips to her, praying she would kiss him back. The cold of her lips finally made the tears in his eyes fall. He pressed his lips a little harder and then pulled back. He turned towards Abby. Her image was broken into a thousand pieces by the water in his eyes. Her sobs sounded broken even more.

"I'm sorry." He said. "She's gone."

She slid beside and past him as she leaned down to her mother's lifeless face. She brushed the hair out of her mother's eyes and kissed her cheek.

"Mom? Don't be gone. You can't be gone. Please don't be gone." She whispered.

"I'm sorry, Abby." He put his hand on her back.

She turned and wrapped her arms around his neck. He felt her shudder as she sobbed into his shoulder. He looked past her at Theresa, and his eyes filled with tears. He closed them and hugged Abby as tight as he could.

He felt Abby shove into him and knock him off balance. Abby's scream added to the sudden confusion. His eyes shot open as she pulled her arms from around his neck. She lurched forward as she awkwardly tried to reach her arms behind herself. She twisted away. He caught a flash of Theresa behind her. She was sitting up. Abby jumped up, still trying to reach her back. She spun again. He could see the hole in her t-shirt and bloom of blood growing around it. He looked back at Theresa. She growled. Their eyes met and his wife lunged towards him. He threw his hands up. "Theresa? THERESA!!" He blocked her with his forearm. Her eyes were pale shells and the gray skin of her face was streaked with tiny blue veins as she snapped her teeth at him.

“GO, RUN!!!” He yelled at Abby.

Abby’s eyes were wide and confused as she stepped past him and ran down the hall. He heard her bedroom door slam shut as the pain erupted in his hand. He jerked his head back and watched his wife’s teeth clamp down around his fingers. The blood spurted from her lips and he felt a bone in his little finger snap. He shoved her in the throat with his other hand, her mouth relaxed. He jerked his hand free. The back of his hand felt like it was on fire.

“STOP IT, THERESA, STOP!!!!” But she didn’t stop.

He backed away from the woman he married as he tried to understand why she was biting at him with every chomp of her jaw. He pushed her hard against the bed and jumped to his feet. The blood from his hand made the floor slick and he almost slipped again. The thing came towards him as he backpedaled through the door. He pulled it shut and stopped. He heard her slam against it. The door shook. The sound of splintering came the second time she slammed into it. He backed down the hallway, pausing just long enough at the bathroom to grab the first aid kit. He knocked on Abby's door. The thing in the master bedroom slammed against the door again but it sounded weaker.

"Abby. Open the door." He said. The lock turned.

"Daddy." She swung the door open and backed away. "What is happening?"

"I don't know honey. I don't know." He shut the door and looked around the room. He grabbed a t-shirt from the closet and began wiping the blood off his hand.

"Mom?"

"That's not your mother. She didn't do this. It's the virus. What they have been talking about on the news. The thing in Madagascar. Marionette." The bite was deep and he could see the bone of his little finger sticking out. He opened the emergency kit and found the splint.

"The rabies thing? Marionette? How did mom get rabies?" She asked.

"Here, take this. You're going to have to fit it around my finger." He said.

"Like this?" She put it against his hand and held it.

"Yeah, but I'm going to straighten it out a little. Just put it around it as soon as I take my hand off and hold it tight until I get the tape on. Okay?" He asked.

"Okay."

He pulled the end of his finger until it somewhat straightened out. The pain was almost more than he could take. He held it in even as he felt himself start to shake. "Put it on." She worked the splint onto the half straight finger. "Hold it tight." He felt her squeeze and he wasn't sure he was going to finish. He steadied himself and wrapped the tape around as tight as what strength he had left let him.

"Okay." He took a deep breath. The sweat dripped from his forehead. "Let me have a second."

"How did mom get rabies?" She asked.

"The wreck. Outside. There was a kid. He bit her."
"Bit her?"

"She didn't want you to worry."

"Daddy, she bit you. She bit me too." Abby said.

"Turn around. Let me see." He said.

She turned and pulled her shirt up. The blood was still fresh. He grabbed the towel hanging on the doorknob and wiped it clean. There was a scoop of flesh missing. But not deep.

"This will sting a little. Sorry that's a lie. It'll sting a lot." He said.

He tore open the alcohol wipe from the kit

and touched it to the wound. She winced. He dabbed until she quit wincing and then he wiped. The large size bandage fit almost perfectly. He added a couple of pieces of tape.

“Okay.” He said.

“Okay?” She asked. “Are we going to be like mom? Are we infected now too?”

“I don’t know.” He said. He looked at her as she sat down on the bed. “I’m sorry.”

“For what?” She asked.

“I didn’t know it had already started.” He said.

“What?”

“I promised your mother I would keep you safe. I promised. But I didn’t know. Didn’t know I’d have to keep you safe from her. I’m sorry.” He felt the tears roll down his cheek.

“Can’t we go to a doctor? Isn’t there something we can do?”

"Is that what you want? Do you want to leave and go try? I'll do whatever you want."

"It won't matter will it?" She asked.

"No, I don't think it would. I'm sorry." He said.

"So we stay here?" She asked.

"If that's what you want."

"With Mom?" She leaned forward and slid off the bed next to him. They both leaned against the wall. He held out his hand.

"With Mom." He said. He wrapped his arm around her.

"So we just wait?" She leaned against him.

"I don't know what else to do. I wish I had been better. I wish I had done better." He said as the tears rolled down his cheek.

"We're all together. I think she would have wanted that." Abby said.

"Yeah, she would have. She loved you so much. I

love you so much. We worked, she worked, so hard to get you here. You are everything we always dreamed of." He said as he brushed the hair out of her eyes.

"She said the same thing. Just before..." She started crying.

"Shh. It's all okay now. We'll rest and we'll wait. And we'll be together." He pulled his arm around her a little tighter and she settled her head against his shoulder. He could hear a cicada buzzing in the morning sun outside the window.

They sat in the bedroom until the sun had left the eastern sky and fell towards the west. He felt her head against his shoulder and opened his eyes. He didn't know how long they had been asleep but he did mark the different angle the light was coming into the room. More than a few minutes for sure. He thought about how long it had taken Theresa to go from bit to biting. A few hours. He looked at Abby's arm but didn't see the ashen color he had seen on Theresa. He lifted his shoulder slightly.

“Hey, wake up.” He whispered. She lifted her head. He looked into her eyes. They were clear.

“How are you feeling?” He asked.

“Okay, I guess.”

“Hand me that mirror off your dresser.” He said. He watched her as she stood. She seemed okay.

“Here.” She said.

He looked at his own reflection and other than the red-rimmed eyes he seemed normal. Maybe in need of a shave but still passable. No ashen skin. No sunken eyes. He handed the mirror back.

“You sure you feel okay?” He asked.

“Yeah, yeah I do.” She said. “What does that mean?”

“I don’t know. Your mother got sick pretty fast.”

He said. “We’ve been asleep at least that long.”

“Maybe we don’t have it. Maybe it goes away. Maybe mom...” She turned towards the door.

He hadn’t expected it so he hesitated. She swung the door open before he could stop her and was down the hall before he could catch up. He came up behind her just as she swung the door to the master bedroom open.

“Mom?” She said.

The thing stood in the middle of the room. The smell of death filled the air. It raised its head at the sound of her voice. He could see the things pale yellow eyes and the ashen, blue veined skin of its face. The lips were pulled back and its teeth were filled with bits of bloody things. Black drool slid from the corner of its mouth onto the floor. He grabbed Abby’s shoulder.

“Stop.” He said. The thing glanced briefly at the sound before its eyes settled back forward.

“Mom?” Abby said again. The thing never moved.

"It's not your mom. She's gone. I'm sorry." He said as he pulled her back into the hallway. He shut the door.

"We have to...." He was interrupted by the sound of a police siren.

For Safekeeping

It was a quick burst. Like a cop trying to get through a red light. Just a quick little half sound but an unmistakable one. He turned and looked out the window. A sheriff's deputy was parked a few yards down the road behind the wrecked car. He could see the door opening.

"Stay here. Stay inside. And don't open that door. No matter what." He pointed at the door he had just shut.

"Okay."

He grabbed the blanket off the back of the couch and wrapped it around himself. The temperature had dropped as the sun slid towards the west. He opened the door. The deputy turned at the sound and reached for his gun.

“Whoa.” Joel raised his hands in the air and the blanket fell away.

“Step outside, sir.” The deputy called.

“Sure.” Joel walked into the yard.

“What happened here sir?” The deputy asked.

“Last night, there was a wreck. We tried to call but there wasn’t any service.” Joel said.

The deputy stepped around the front of the car and the small body in the road moved.

“Watch out. I don’t...” Joel started to yell. The sound of the pistol shot blasted through his ears. The thing in the road jerked backwards and its head disintegrated on the asphalt.

“Jesus.” Joel said.

“That’s the fifth one so far.” The deputy said.

“Fifth one?”

“Dead thing I’ve had to shoot.” The deputy said.

“Dead thing?”

“I don’t know how else to put it. They should all be dead. Wrecked, shot, stabbed, burnt and all past the point they should be alive. They can’t be alive. They have to be dead. But I have to keep shooting them. I have to keep shooting them all.” He said as he stared down at the thing in the road.

“Are you okay?”

“Yeah. Yeah.” He shook his head and looked at Joel. “How about you? What happened to your hand?” He nodded.

Joel looked down at the t-shirt wrapped around his hand. It was bloody. He held it up.

“Busted it last night. The power went out when this happened.” He motioned at the wreck. “I got out of bed and tripped. Fell into the mirror on the dresser." He stopped himself. He knew that too much detail would just as telling as too little. His penchant for detective novels was paying off.

"You need some help? I have a good first aid kit." The deputy started walking to the back of his patrol car.

"No, no. I'm fine. We'll probably head to the hospital and get it looked at." Joel said.

"Hospital?" The deputy said. "There ain't no hospital. There ain't nothing."

"What do you mean there ain't nothing?" Joel asked. "What's going on out there?"

"Out there? Jesus man, it's right here. Did you not just see that shit right there? I had to shoot that thing because it wouldn't die. And that is happening everywhere. Everything is dying. But the dead won't stay dead. All over the city, all over the country, hell, all over the world."

"What are we supposed to do?" Joel asked.

"The army began broadcasting on all the police bands a few hours ago. They are talking about refugee centers. There's one out at Stone Mountain."
"We'd have to cross half the city."

"There's another one west, towards the state line. It's a lot further but there's not a couple million people between here and there." The deputy said. "Can you help us?" He asked.

"Nope. I'm officially retired. I decided to take the patrol car, the weapons and anything else I went to work with yesterday evening with me as a pension. I got a tank a gas, another ten gallons in the trunk, a load of food and I am getting as far away from people as I can." The deputy said.

"Why?" Joel asked.

"Because people are the problem. The infection spreads through biting. Scratching. Hell maybe breathing for all they know. All I know is the fewer people, the fewer infected trying to infect me." The deputy said. "But I will help you a tiny bit."

"How so?"

"I can see that hand." The deputy said. "I can see the bone sticking out of the side of that splint."

"Yeah. It's pretty bad."

"Here." He handed him a small bag from the large medical toolbox in his trunk.

"What's this?"

"It's a local anesthetic. Just use the little syringe and jab it around it. It'll deaden it."

"For what?"

"You're gonna have to cut it off. There ain't no setting that back. Better to cut it off, wrap it up and use the antibiotics in this bag and hope it doesn't get infected." The deputy handed him another bag.

"Cut it off?"

"If you don't, it will definitely get infected. And you'll run out of antibiotics. And then you'll die.

Cut it off and wrap it up. It'll be better. But your call." The deputy said.

"So that's it?" Joel asked.

"I guess. More than I intended when I stopped." The deputy tossed his hat into the passenger seat.

"Thank you. My name's Joel. Joel Patterson. Maybe I can pay you back someday." Joel said.

"Maybe. Goodbye Joel. Hope you make it." The deputy slid into the seat. The car pulled away.

He watched the car pull around the bend and disappear. He stood in the yard for another minute listening. He could still hear sirens blaring towards downtown. He heard helicopters in the distance. He turned and went back in the house.

"Abby?" He looked into the living room. "Abby?" He turned towards the kitchen. He spun around. "ABBY!!!" He ran to the bedroom. The door was open.

Abby stood in front of the thing. It hadn't

moved from where he had last seen it.

“Abby.” He whispered harshly.

“She won’t do anything.” Abby said as she looked at the woman in front of her. “She looks like Mom, but it’s not her. Maybe it’s her body but her spirit is gone or something.”

“It’s not your mother.” He said. He slowly stepped into the room. The thing stood almost motionless except for a slight rocking of its head like a baby that has just about mastered holding its head up.

“She’s different.” Abby said.

“Different?” Joel stepped a little closer.

“When she bit us she was angry. Like a rage or something. Now she’s practically asleep.” Abby said. “Like she doesn’t even know we’re here. Look.” Abby poked the things arm. It didn’t react.

“Abby stop.” He stepped beside her.

“What does it mean?” Abby asked.

"What does what mean?"

"This. All this. Why is she different? Or is there something different about us?" She asked. "I mean shouldn't we be like her by now?"

"Like her?" Joel tilted his head.

"Yeah, it's been almost all day now. And we're both still okay. Shouldn't we have, I don't know, turned into that by now?" Abby pointed.

He wasn't ready to answer her question. He didn't have an answer. But she was right. Something was different. They should be at least feeling sick or something. Something.

"We have to leave." He said. "We have to go."

"Why?"

"Because we can't stay here and the sooner we get going, the better it will be." He said.

"Okay. What about her?" She asked.

"I don't know. We'll figure that out. Right now we

need to get some things together." He said as he turned towards the door. She paused, looking closely at the woman in front of her, and then turned and followed. She shut the door behind her. He led her into the kitchen.

"We need to get all the food worth carrying together. I'll try to see if I can dig out some backpacks." He said.

"Okay."

"But first, I'm going to need you to do something."

"What?" She asked.

He held up one of the bags the deputy had given him.

"I'm going to need you to, well, I'm going to need your help." He smiled.

"Okay."

Two hours later and he still couldn't feel

anything. He had jabbed all around his hand because he didn't think it was working. It was working. He hadn't felt anything at all. He had ended up having her stretch his finger out so he could snip the broken part off with the wire cutters. The short end of the bone was just under the surface of the remainder of his finger. He had wrapped everything up tight. He had enough bandages to redress it several times and enough antibiotics to fight off all but the worst infections. The queasiness that settled in his stomach as he cut his own finger off had waned. She had seemed morbidly fascinated as she helped him. The blood didn't seem to bother her as much as it had him.

"You could be a doctor." He said as she plopped down on the couch next to him. "Really, you could."

"I didn't do anything." She said. She popped open the bag of chips.
"You did a lot. And you did it well. I couldn't have done that at your age. I would've passed out or something." He said.

"Whatever." She smiled. "Want one?" She tilted the bag towards him. He took one. He smiled at her as he chewed.

A few hours later he sat against the side of the couch and listened to her sleep. The day had turned to night and was starting to turn into day again. He had almost forgotten about the thing that used to be his wife in the back bedroom. He dozed in and out as the pain in his hand waxed and waned. He had taken the last two pills in the bottle from his dentist. The fog in his head was not quite as thick as the fog outside. He stood and looked at the ghostly sphere of the sun through the thick gray clouds that came up from the ground. He heard her stir.

"I think we've got everything packed." He said.

"Do we need to load it into the car?" She asked.

"Not yet. I think we'll stay another day. The fog is pretty thick. And I really don't want to leave unless we have a clear morning. I think we're safe here for another night." He said.

"Why do we have to leave?"

"We could stay. But we'd run out of food. We'd run out of water. And then we'd run out of chances." He said.

"How do you know what we'll find out there?"

"The deputy said the army was setting up refugee centers. We're going to get to one."

"Where?"

"Towards Alabama. He didn't say for sure. We'll make our way on the back roads but we'll be following the interstate. I know those roads pretty good and I've got a good map. If there's a refugee center we're sure to find it. And that's where we'll find help." He said.

"So what do we do today?" She asked.

"Listen to the radio. Make sure we have what we need." He said.

"How far is this place?" She asked.

"I don't know for sure. But it's only a few hours to the state line." He asked.

"Why do we need all this stuff then if it's just a few hours?" She asked.

"Maybe we won't but I don't think getting there is going to be as easy as it used to be. It will be dangerous so we'll have to take our time. And if it gets too dangerous, we may have to think of something else." He said.

"What else?" She asked.

"I don't know. But that's why we need all this stuff." He said.

They spent the day getting their backpacks ready, adjusting the straps and moving things from hers to his until they both were comfortable with what they had to carry if they had to walk. Joel remembered the camping trips with his father and the excitement of getting everything together the day before. He didn't feel excitement as he helped her take the pack off. He sat it against the wall and turned to her. "Get some rest." He said. He didn't feel excitement at all, he felt afraid.

The air was cool. He looked up at the clear sky and saw a few streaks of light. Nothing like the night before last. Or was it the night before that? So much, so fast. He sat the can down next to the side of the house and threw the blankets off his back onto the ground. Satisfied, he walked back around to the front of the house. He thought about Theresa. His knees weakened and he lowered his gaze from the sky. He felt warm tears on his cheeks. He looked up again. The sky was broken through the water in his eyes. He wiped them and turned.

He slid by the couch. Abby was snoring a little as he slipped down the hallway to the spare bedroom. More moving boxes were still stacked in the corner. He pulled the top box off and dumped the clothes on the floor and walked over to the window. He unlatched the lock. The last thing was to move the wooden chair in the other corner on top of the clothes scattered in the room. He stepped back into the hallway and closed the door. He stood in front of the door to the master bedroom for a few seconds listening to the sound of his own breathing. He opened the door.

The room felt colder. The thing stood in the same spot it had been in for two days. He stepped in front of it but the eyes were vacant and didn't even move when he came closer. He reached his hand out and touched her arm. No reaction. He tilted his head a little as he closed his eyes. He gently stroked her arm. He tried to remember the smile on her face and the life in her eyes. Tears squeezed between his lids.

"I don't..." His voice cracked. "I don't know what this is, I don't know what this means but I want to believe this is you. I want to believe she's okay because you loved her so much you couldn't hurt her. I want to believe that if there is anything left of you in there, it is fighting like hell to keep her safe. I want you to hear me. You don't have to fight anymore. You can rest. I will fight for both of us now. I will keep her safe. I will fight just like you. Until I can't fight any more. I love you." He paused. The thing was still staring into nothing and had not moved. He leaned closer. "I love you." He gently kissed the things forehead. "Goodbye."

He turned and walked out the door. The hallway was a little brighter and he could see gray light coming through the windows in the living room. He heard her stirring.

"It's time." He said.
"I'm ready." She said. "I want to say goodbye."

"No." He said. "That's not your mother."

"Can I see her?"

"Remember her like she was. Not like this." He said. "Here, I took this from her nightstand. It's from your birthday last year." He handed her a picture of the three of them.

She looked at the picture. The smile on her mother's face, a half crooked smirk, made a tear come to her eye.

"You're right. That's not mom." She said as she hugged him. "Maybe one day when this is all over we'll come back, and she'll still be there. Just waiting."

They loaded the backpacks into the backseat. He grabbed the box of tools from the bench in the back of the garage and a set of jumper cables hanging from a hook. He tossed it in the trunk. They climbed into the car and he backed out of the driveway. He paused and put the car in park.

"Hold on one second." He said.

"What?"

"Just going to make sure the gas line to the house is turned off. It's on the other side of the house. Just take a second." He jumped out of the car and disappeared around the side of the house.

He tossed the blankets into the open window, draping the last one on the window ledge. He leaned through the window and doused everything he could with gasoline before pouring the last few drops on the blanket draped outside. He flicked the lighter and the gasoline caught. The fire leapt into the room as he jogged back to the car. He had never burnt a house down before so he wasn't sure it would work. He pulled onto the road and accelerated. He didn't tell her. He would let her always believe that her mother was forever in that room, in that house, waiting. The dark smoke rising above the trees in the rearview mirror told him the truth.

The Other End of the Road

The pickup truck blocked the road. Joel leaned forward and looked through the windshield at the four men standing in front of him. He looked over at Abby before he rolled down the window.

"Where are you going?" The man asked from behind the sunglasses.

"West. Trying to find the refugee center." Joel said.

"Where are you coming from?" The man asked.

"Atlanta. North Atlanta." Joel said.

"Going the wrong way ain't you? Stone Mountain

is east." The man said.

"Yeah, but I heard there was a refugee center west. And I didn't want to go through the city." Joel said.

The man leaned into the car.

"Young lady, do you know this man?" The man asked.

"Huh?" She asked.

"This man, do you know him?"

"He's my dad."

"You sure?"

"He's my dad."

"What kind of question is that?" Joel asked.

"Bad times, bad people take advantage of them. Always have, always will." The man said.

"And you think I'm bad people?"

"Didn't say one way or the other, that's why I asked." The man said.

“I can just turn around.” Joel said.

“No need. We’ll take you through.” The man said as he turned and snapped his finger at one of the other men.

“Through?” Joel asked.

“Yeah, through. You get behind Willie here and stay behind him. He’ll take you to the other end town and you can be on your way.” The man said.

“Why?”

“Why what?”

“I don’t know, why are you escorting us? Why are you letting us through? A whole lotta why.” Joel said.

“We’re escorting you because we are letting you through. We’re letting you through because you need to get to the other side of our town. I would rather know you came and went than wait around for you to try another way to get through.” The man said.

"Why are you doing all this?" Joel asked.

"Where did you say you was coming from?"

"Atlanta."

"Do you really need to ask why we're doing all this?" The man leaned into the window.

"No, no I guess I don't." Joel said.

"You stay behind Willie and be sure to not come this way again. You understand?" The man said as he waved at the truck in front of Joel.

"Yeah, I understand." Joel followed the truck.

The little town looked deserted. He could see curtains moving and little slits in blinds closing as they drove by. The truck passed by the courthouse and Joel could see a few people standing on the steps shielding their eyes in the sun. He followed the truck until the trees once again came to the side of the road. Another few trucks were parked in the road ahead but they parted as his car approached. The man he had followed pulled over to the side of the road. Joel watched the trucks pull back across the road in the rearview mirror as they drove on.

“That was weird.” Abby said as she looked behind them.

“Yeah, but it could have been worse.” He said.

“It was a little scary.” She said. He drove another mile, watching the mirror the whole way. Finally he pulled the car over and stopped.

“What are we doing?”

“Just a quick stop. Stay in the car. Just gotta get something from the trunk.” He said as he exited the car.

“Okay.”

He stood in the road and listened. The sound of sirens was gone. He could hear the wind, some birds and off in the distance the sound of helicopters. He looked up and down the road. Nothing moved. He opened the trunk and unzipped the bag. The pistol had been his father's. It was an old 357 police revolver. His father had bought it at an auction at least ten years ago. He had given it to Joel for safekeeping when he started getting confused. Joel had shot it a few times and although he didn't know much about pistols, the guys that took him to shoot seemed impressed both with the firearm and Joel's natural talent for hitting the target. He knew how to shoot rifles, bows, shotguns and more but handguns had just never been his thing. He picked it up. It felt heavier than he remembered. He flipped the cylinder open. Loaded. He rummaged around the bag and found the half box of ammo. He slid the bag off the case underneath and undid the latches. It had been over a year since he had shot it but he hoped the scope was still close. He grabbed the box of rifle ammo and closed the trunk.

"Here." He handed her the ammo. "Put it in the glove box."

"What about that?" She pointed to the rifle on his shoulder.

"You remember how it works?"

"I think so."

"Watch." He worked the bolt half back. He could see the rounds in the magazine. "Just pull this all the way back and push it forward. Lock it down like this. This is the safety. It's loaded now. So don't mess with it." Joel said as he put it across the back seat. "I'm going to keep this right here." He shoved the pistol down between the seats. "Don't mess with it either. Understand?"

"Understand." She said. "Why do we need guns, Dad?" She asked.

"I hope we don't. But I can't lie to you. Things are getting really dangerous. People are going to panic. They already are. And people are dangerous when they panic. We're going to try to avoid the panic." He said.

"And if we can't?" She asked.

"That's what we might need the guns for." He said. "Ready?"

"Yeah."

They drove down empty two-lane roads. The map was a book of atlases of the south. It was a few years old but most of the roads they were on had been here for decades. Not a lot of updates to make on the maps. It even mapped some of the unpaved roads that wound through the wildest parts. He used those to avoid anything that looked like a town. He chose roads that crossed the interstate but didn't access the interstate. He knew any road that accessed the interstate would go nowhere fast. Even on the mostly deserted back roads they had to turn around twice when wrecks blocked their way. They only stopped when he was sure there were no other people around. When they crossed a bridge over the interstate they stopped. The traffic below was all headed away from Atlanta but it was at a stand still. There were things moving inside and outside the cars. The smell was overpowering in the unusually warm autumn day.

"They're all infected aren't they?" She asked.

“Yeah, I think they are.” He replied.

“Were they all trying to go where we’re going?” Abby asked.

“I don’t know.” He said.

“Do you think it’s really out there? The place we’re going?” She asked.

“I don’t know.” He said.

“We’re going to keep trying aren’t we?”

“Yeah, we’re going to keep trying. We’re always going to keep trying.” He said. “Let’s go.”

She shifted in the seat. He looked over at her.

“You think there’s anything on the radio?” She asked.

They had tried when they first pulled away from the house but there wasn’t much but static and the constant Emergency Message. She scanned the channels.

"This is an emergency......Please stay tuned for...The President has been moved...."

"Wait, turn it back. That was new." He said.

"...secure location. The Vice President is en route to Cheyenne Mountain according to sources familiar with the situation. Once again the Department of Justice has affirmed that protecting life and limb falls well within the right of self-defense. The National Institute of Health has determined that the infection is irreversible and that all efforts should be made to avoid any contact with the infected. Local authorities should use all necessary force to protect citizens from infected persons. The Attorney General, in a statement as he boarded an Air Force aircraft at Joint Base Andrews said, and I quote, 'If anyone thinks I'm going to prosecute someone for killing one of these infected sons-a-bitches, they need to find another AG.'

An audible breath was heard through the radio

"Ladies and gentlemen of the listening audience forgive me a bit of editorializing right now but the statements I just read to you are remarkable. I am reminded of a quote from Lenin, 'there are decades when nothing happens and weeks when decades happen.' I don't know what happens now but based on what has happened so far, I fear we are in the infancy of what is to come. Be careful and may we all stay safe."

He turned the radio off. As they wound their way through the countryside, she drifted back to sleep. The clouds that hung low over the trees slowly turned gray. As the car came around the long curve, the trees fell away to a wide expanse of valley below. He slammed on the brakes.

"What?" She said after she snapped back in the seat. "What's happening?" She blinked hard.

"Sorry. Sorry. Look." He pointed to the valley below. A helicopter slowly lifted off the ground.

They both got out of the car. The interstate

was a few miles in the distance on the other side of the compound. There was a road, hastily constructed that looked mostly to be red clay and gravel. It ran from the interstate exit ramp down to a big gate. The entire area was fenced.

“What is that place?” She asked.

“It was a warehouse farm.” He said.

“A what?”

“Just a bunch of warehouses all together. Bunch of companies rent space in them. It’s like a central distribution hub for businesses that don’t have a distribution hub in the area.” He said.

“How do you know so much?” She asked.

“The magazine did an article about who was buying land up and down the interstate. Kind of a ‘did you ever wonder?’ thing. I had to play editor on it. I guess the army took it over. Look.” He pointed at the road coming from the interstate. There were several military vehicles parked at the gate. He could see the fence around the warehouses but there was another fence beyond that. It formed an empty space around the whole compound and he could see soldiers walking in the space between.

“How did they build it so fast?” She asked.

“It’s what they do I guess. We need to figure a way down there. I don’t think we’re going to be able to get to that road from here.”

“If we can see it from here,” She said. “We can walk.”

“Walk? You sure?” He asked.

“That’s where we need to go right?”

“I think so. I mean it looks like a refugee center to me.” He said.

“Well let’s walk.” She reached into the back and grabbed one of the backpacks.

“Okay. Get everything we can carry. I don’t think we’ll be coming back.” He said.

He looked in the glove box again. The registration and the owner's manual were all that was left. He patted the roof of the car.

"You've been a good one. Hate to leave you here." He said.

"It's just a car dad."

"I know. But it has been a good one." He said. "Ready?"

"Yep."

They stepped over the guardrail and started down the long slope through the trees to the open space below. The trees swallowed them as they walked. He figured it was a mile through the woods to get to where they had seen the refugee camp. Leaves littered the ground and more dropped as the breeze blew. The sun flickered in and out of the ones still clinging to the branches and he could hear the steady buzz of insects and frogs. The sound of the woods. He touched her shoulder.

"Nice huh?" He looked around.

"I guess. You know it's not really my thing." She said. "Too many crawly things."

"You just helped me cut off my finger and you're worried about crawly things?" He smiled.

"That was different." She said.

"If you say so." He said.

They walked through the woods on the freshly fallen leaves. The sound of helicopters came and went in the distance and he occasionally he heard the sound of a car horn. He could see the trees beginning to thin in front of them. She walked ahead.

"Dad, look." She pointed ahead and started moving faster.

He could see the edge of the trees and a few people standing out in the open. They both quickened their pace. She broke through the trees just ahead of him and reached out to the man standing in front of her.

"Hey, mister is that the refugee camp?" She asked as she touched his shoulder.

The thing turned. Its face was ashen. Joel could see the little blue veins running up the side of its neck.

"Stop." He grabbed her shoulder.

The thing looked at her, then at him. Then its eyes just looked ahead. Joel looked at the other people standing in the field between them and the gate. All of them were slowly shuffling towards the fence.

"Don't move." He said. "They are all infected."

She stopped.

"What do we do?" She started to back up.

"I don't know. Stay here." He said.

"No."

"Just stay here. I'm going to try something. If

something happens, run to the car. Find another way to the camp." He said.

"Run back to the car? Find another way? Not without you I won't." She said.

"Listen to me. One day you'll have to make your way without me. You have to know that. And you have to be able to do it. I won't be here forever." He said.

"No, but you don't have to do something stupid." She said.

"Just wait here. Okay?" He said.

"Okay. But I'm not leaving you." She said.

"Fine."

He dropped his backpack and stepped forward. He went past the first infected, maybe it wasn't completely infected or something he thought, and walked towards a group of three of them. He closed his eyes and took a deep breath. "Please let me be right." He whispered under his breath. He stepped in front of the group.

The eyes were all the same. Pale with some kind of haze over them, like dirty windows. The one closest to him barely turned towards his movement. He reached out and touched the things arm. It didn't react. There was a vicious tear along the side of the things face and the skin fell in a flap under its jaw. He could see the white bone underneath the black rot dripping from the hole. The other two didn't move at all other than the slow steady shuffle towards the fence and the constant chomping teeth, as though they were taking bites of the air.

He looked back at Abby. She stood still. He walked back over to her and grabbed his backpack.

"I think we can get through them. I don't think they know we're here." He said.

"Why did the radio tell people to avoid them? They don't seem dangerous." She said as they started forward.

“They’re dangerous. They showed things on the television. Attacks.” He said.

“Then why aren’t they attacking us?” She asked.

“I don’t know. Be careful. Slow.” He said.

They walked gingerly around the group of three. Beyond that there were more. A lot more. They approached the back of the largest crowd. The smell was both distinct and overpowering. He covered his mouth.

“Look.” She pointed.

He followed her finger. The fence was still several hundred yards away but he could see the guard tower. He could make out someone looking at them through binoculars. He waved. The man with the binoculars waved back.

Red Flag

"Sergeant I need you to make sure that we can get that next layer of fencing up tonight." The major said without looking up.

"Yes sir. We should have the entire eastern side completed by zero four thirty." Sergeant Ponzi replied.

"You and your men have been invaluable. How much longer is General Eckerd going to let you TDY with me?" The major asked.

"Sir as far as I know we're yours until we get a Red Flag." Ponzi said.

“Good. Let’s go for a walk.” The major stood. The tent flap was half open and they both stepped into the sunlight. Ponzi put on his sunglasses.

“Sergeant this isn’t going to hold. No matter what we do. You know it, I know it.”

“Yes sir.”

“What would you do?”

“Excuse me sir?”

“What would you do with the people here? The people still stuck out there trying to get here. What do they think we are capable of? They can see can’t they?” The major pointed at the interstate overpass in the distance.

“It’s all they know. Someone else will fix it. Just go where you’re told to go, do what you’re told to do and everything will be fine. Funny thing sir, ninety-nine out of a hundred times, they’re right. Maybe they are a bunch of sheep but it’s still kinda rare for the entire herd to go flying off the cliff.” Ponzi said.

“Until now.” The major said.

“Yeah, well rare ain’t never, sir.”

“So what would you do?”

“Sir what chance do those people out there have? Fifty-fifty?” Ponzi asked.

“Maybe. Probably less.”

“But without us, they have none. With us here they have something to fight for. As long as we hold out they will fight to get here. We’re a goal. Most of them won’t make it. I know what it looks like when it gets really bad. And we don’t even know what we’re fighting. I’ve heard that you ain’t even gotta get bit to turn into one of those things. Guy in aviation said they picked up a family on an ambulance run this morning. The man had a massive heart attack. Medic said they thought he was dead when they got him on the helo. Said the guy woke up while they were in flight. Went crazy. They tried to restrain him but couldn’t. Bit the medic, bit his own wife. Both of them are in the medical tent right now."

"What happened to the guy?" The major asked.

"They didn't have a choice but dump him out the door at altitude while his kid watched."

"Jesus." The major said.

"Point is sir, this is all we can do. There are no good options left. And when there are no good options left, you fight. That's it." Ponzi said.

"Have you seen one? Up close?"

"Not really." Ponzi said.

"Come with me."

The major led him around the back of the tent. The landing area was about fifty yards across. The big Chinook sat on the ground with its rotors rocking gently in the breeze. The smaller Blackhawk was en route to the Stone Mountain station to retrieve another load of medications. They walked past the guard stationed at the back of the Chinook.

“Everything good corporal?” The major asked.

“Yes sir.”

“They started the poker game yet, Shrek?” Ponzi asked.

“Not yet Sergeant. But I’m busted. My wife will kill me if I lose any more money.” Corporal Meyers said.

“Well, I can spot you a fifty.”

“I’m good. Besides, I got a feeling we’re gonna Red Flag out of here tonight, anyway.”

“Oh you got a feeling do ya?” Ponzi said.

“Heard they popped one at Stone Mountain this morning. Said they went south. Towards the coast.” Meyers said.

“I could handle a little beach time. Maybe you’re right. Stay sharp, until that next section of fence is up things could still go tits up real fast.”

“Will do Sergeant.” Meyers said.

“Carry on Corporal.” The major said.

“Yes sir.” Meyers saluted.

The major returned the salute as he ducked under the stabilizer on the side of the aircraft. They walked to the other side of the landing zone and beyond the portable toilets set up at the very back of the fenced in area.

“Where are we going sir?” Ponzi asked.

“Right over here.” The major pointed at to the watchtower. They walked to a small gate the patrols used to get in and out of the no-man’s-land. The private on duty opened the gate. They walked across the open area to the base of the tower. They didn’t go up. The major took him right to the outer fence.

There were a half dozen infected on the other side. As they approached, the sounds of growls and groans filled the air. One slammed his head against the chain link as it tried to clamp its teeth into the steel. Rot splattered on the ground in front of them.

"Close enough?" The major said.

"Yeah, uh yes sir. Jesus." Ponzi said.

"I don't think this is the Messiah." The major said. "But I do think he has been resurrected."

"And the sea gave up the dead who were in it, and Death and Hell delivered up the dead who were in them. And they were judged." Ponzi said.

"Revelations 20." The major said. "Didn't figure you for a religious man Sergeant."

"Italian, Catholic." Ponzi said.

"You believe it?"

"What's that sir?"

"Do you believe it? Revelations?" The major asked.

"I don't know. It always struck me like it was more to make an impression than a prediction."

"And now?"

“Maybe I was wrong.” Ponzi said.

“Let’s go up top.” The major and Ponzi climbed the watchtower stairs. The two soldiers on duty stepped aside as they looked over the edge. “Maybe a hundred so far. More show up every hour. I don’t think we can hold this very long if they keep coming.” The major said. “We will either have to leave or we have to reduce their numbers.”

“Reduce their numbers?” Ponzi asked.

“We may not have a choice.” The major said as he raised the binoculars to his eyes. “The infected are a threat.”

“Are you suggesting we just start shooting them? Where they stand?” Ponzi asked.

“Would you rather wait until we have to?” The major said.

“Sir, I understand the ROE. I understand if threatened we can engage with lethal force to reduce the threat. I don’t think a bunch of unarmed civilians, even infected ones, are enough of a threat to warrant mass executions."

"You really think that thing at the fence is just an unarmed civilian? You aren't seeing the truth Sergeant." The major said.

"What is the truth sir?" Ponzi asked.

"The truth? What is out there is neither a citizen nor is it unarmed. You've read the reports. You've seen the videos. Does that really look like someone with a cold? They attack, they kill, they infect, they move on. The truth is Sergeant they're already dead. They died and they came back.

"Died and came back?" Ponzi said. "Are you serious? Sir."

"This is how it ends Sergeant." The major held the binoculars as he spoke. "Sergeant?" He asked.

"Yes sir?"

"Remind me again what your Red Flag order says." The major asked without lowering the binoculars.

"The BOLO is for anyone that exhibits atypical

behavior around the infected."

"And atypical would be?" The major asked.

"Hell if I know."

"How about walking through a bunch of them without getting attacked? Would that be atypical?"

"I think it would, why?"

"I'm going to hate to say this because I know that I'm going to lose the most effective part of what little defense we have left but I think you're about to have your Red Flag. Look." He handed Ponzi the binoculars. "Just this side of that stand of trees, coming across the field." He pointed.

Ponzi put the binoculars to his eyes and searched for what the major wanted him to see. The man was probably forty or so and the girl a teenager. He watched them moved through a group of infected like they were passing on the sidewalk. None of the infected reacted. The girl raised her hand and pointed towards the watchtower. The man looked where the girl pointed and waved his hand. Ponzi waved back. He thumbed the mike on his earpiece.

"Angel two angel two this is Madoff. Red Flag, Red Flag, Red Flag."

He climbed down the ladder and went to the fence. As he waited for the two people he had seen crossing the field to arrive, he could hear the helicopter spinning up behind him.

Where it all Began

“What happened to your hand?” The woman in the mask asked as she cleaned it and applied a couple of stitches.
“It was an accident. I tripped.” He lied.

“You don’t have to lie. There’s nothing to fear.” She said. She lowered the mask and smiled. “If you have been bitten, you need to tell me.”

“Fine. But it was three days ago. I’m not sick at all.” He said.

“How were you bitten? Were you in contact with

an infected?" She asked.

"Yeah, my wife." He lowered his head.

"Your daughter as well?" She asked.
"Yes." He said.
"Where is your wife now?" She asked.

"We left her. She's gone." He said.

"I understand." The woman said. "I'm sorry."

"Thank you." He said. "I need to see my daughter."

"Come with me." The woman said.

Joel stood. He looked around the warehouse. It was almost empty. There were two people lying on cots on the other side of the partition with two soldiers standing watch. He could see the handcuffs holding them to the cots. They walked out of the rolling door.

"Dad." Abby said from the entrance of the building across the little muddy patch. She ran to him.

"Abby, are you okay?" He asked.

"Yeah." She hugged him.

Two more soldiers came around the side.

"I need you to come with us. Both of you." The soldier said.

"Where are we going?" Joel said.

"Are those your things?" The other soldier pointed at the backpacks against the side of the building. The pistol and rifle were laid on top of them.

"Yes." Joel said.

"Grab them, you'll need to bring all your things." The soldier said.

Joel and Abby grabbed the backpacks and put them on. He held the pistol out to the soldier.

"You don't want it?" The soldier asked.

"I wasn't sure if I could keep it."

"You better. You may need it." The soldier said. "Come with us."

They started walking. Joel could hear the thunderous whisper of the jet engine on the Chinook singing. They walked towards the helicopter.

“Where are we going?” Joel asked again.

“Honestly I don’t know. But you and your daughter are now my responsibility to get you there.” The soldier said.

“If you don’t know where we’re going, how do you know how to get us there?” Abby asked.

“Who are you?” Joel asked.

“I am Sergeant Michael Ponzi. This is Corporal Meyers. Call him Shrek, he loves that.” Ponzi smiled at Meyers.

“I’m Joel Patterson and this is my daughter Abby. What is this all about Sergeant?” He asked.

“You.” Ponzi said. “You and your daughter.”

“I don’t understand.”

"You fit the parameters. You and your daughter walked through a bunch of infected without so much as a whisper. That qualifies as unusual behavior. And my orders are to transport those who exhibit unusual behavior around the infected to somewhere else." Ponzi said.

"Where is that?" Joel asked.

"I don't know. I won't know until we're in the air. Operational security."

"What if we don't want to go?" Abby asked.

"Mam, at this point, you don't have a choice. Besides, staying here is bad news. This place won't last a week the way things are going." Meyers said.

"But it's safe?" Joel asked. "Where we're going, it's safe?"

"Safer than this place." Meyers said.

"That's enough Corporal." Ponzi said. "Sir, we're under orders to transport you and that is what we're going to do. Is that going to be a problem?"

Ponzi glanced at the pistol stuffed in Joel's belt.

Joel looked at him and followed his gaze down to the gun. He looked up.

"No. No problem. I just need to know my daughter is going to be safe." Joel said.

"I can promise you this, that bird right there doesn't have any infected on it and it will be a few thousand feet above any infected down here. Right now, that's about as safe as you can get." Ponzi said as he pointed to the Chinook.

"And when we land?" Joel asked.

"I guess we'll find out together." Ponzi said.

A squad of four more soldiers stood at the ramp of the helicopter. The blades were turning slowly but he could hear the whine of the engine. They walked up the ramp. The two soldiers and the squad that greeted them followed them on board. He had never been on a helicopter. He had never been around any real military equipment, unless the old tank in Memorial Park counted. It was loud. The steel floor felt unnatural under his feet. The soldiers walked normally but he felt himself feeling unsure, as though it was slippery but it wasn't. Maybe it was the vibration coming through the aircraft, maybe it was his imagination. The seats were heavy netting wrapped around a steel frame. They set their backpacks in the middle of the aircraft and sat down. The helicopter got louder. He felt it start to lift. He looked through the little porthole window and then at Abby. She was looking through the other window. He tapped her shoulder and smiled.

"We'll be okay." He said. Maybe he convinced her, he still wasn't sure. He turned to the soldiers seated across from them.

"So we're up. Where..." He started.

The soldier shook his head and reached behind him to grab a headset hanging on the wall. He pointed over Joel's shoulder. Joel turned and saw another headset hanging behind him. He took it and put it on.

“Can you hear me?” Joel said into the mic.

“Go ahead.” The voice in ear said. The soldier put his thumb up as he spoke.

“We’re up, where are we going?” Joel asked.

“Don’t know yet. The pilot said he would let me know when they told him.” Ponzi said.

“Who are they?” Joel asked.

“Just sit back and relax. You’ll get answers when we get where we’re going?”

“And that is?” Joel asked.

Ponzi looked out the window. “South.” He said.

Joel put the headphones back on the hook and leaned back. He reached over and held his daughter’s hand.

“What did they say?” Abby asked.

“They said we’re going to be safe.” Joel answered.

The helicopter banked into the sun and the

portholes cast beams of light across the cabin. He watched the dust swirl. The ramp they had boarded on was not completely closed. The air was chilly but waves of heat from the exhaust swept through when the helicopter tilted one way or another.

"You awake back their?" The pilots voice came through Ponzi's headset.

"Not really." Ponzi said.

"Well, wake up. We have a target and follow-on. I think you're going to like it." The pilot said.

"Yeah, why's that?"

"Per General Eckerd, 'Transport HVP to Navarre Station for delivery to project. Proceed to USS Ronald Reagan at given coordinates.' It's sitting in the Gulf." The pilot said.

"Wait so we drop these folks and then head to a carrier in the Gulf? Away from all this shit?" Ponzi asked.

“That’s what the man said.” The pilot said.

“Well hell flyboy, doesn’t this thing go any faster?” Ponzi smiled.

“We’re wide ass open right now. We should reach Navarre Station in about thirty minutes.” The pilot said. “As soon as you can get our guests to un-ass the platform, we’ll be sipping drinks on a boat.”

“You get me on the ground, I’ll get them out the door.” Ponzi said.

Joel watched Ponzi having his conversation. He saw him look their way and smile several times. Maybe it was good news. Joel grabbed the headset.

“Any news?” Joel asked.

Ponzi held his hand up and Joel watched him switch over to the cabin channel.
“Say again.” Ponzi said.

“I asked if there was any news.” Joel said.

“Yeah, you’re going to Navarre Station just outside of Pensacola.” Ponzi said.

“And what happens when we get there?” Joel asked.

“We leave.” Ponzi said.

“That’s it? What is there? What happens when you leave?” Joel felt a little panic rise inside his chest.

“That’s all I know.” Ponzi said.

“Can’t you tell me anything else? I have to make sure my daughter is safe.” Joel said.

“I can’t tell you what I don’t know. You are high value personnel and we are under orders to deliver you to Navarre Station. I guess you’ll figure out the rest when you get there.”

“Where are you going after you’ve delivered us to wherever the hell you said?” Joel asked.

“That’s classified.” Ponzi said. “And that’s all I know. Sit back, we’ll be there in half an hour.”

Joel took the headphones off again. Abby was turned around in her seat watching the world go by through the window. He smiled at her. He could feel the soldier watching him. He glanced down at the pistol. That was a non-starter and he knew it. He was not going to change what was going to happen. The feeling of helplessness began to creep over him again. Had he failed? Was going to the refugee camp just the last in the long line of mistakes he had made in the last few days? A wave of fear and panic swept over him when Abby turned in her seat.

“They’re flying over the ocean, look.” She smiled.

He swallowed hard and turned to look. The aircraft was out over the beach but turning back towards land. He felt the helicopter begin to settle towards the ground. When the wheels touched back to earth, he felt sick. Ponzi and another soldier stood. They grabbed Joel and Abby’s backpacks and waited for the ramp to lower. They tossed the packs on the ground outside the helicopter. Ponzi turned to Joel and yelled.

“This is where you get off.” He said.

“But what is out there?” Joel asked.

He looked out the back of the helicopter but didn’t see anything but a fence. The field looked like the same one they just left from but it wasn’t.

“Where are we? What is this place?” Joel yelled.

“Navarre Station. You have to get off. Now.” Ponzi pointed down the ramp.

“No. Not until you tell us what this place is.” Joel demanded.

Ponzi pulled out his pistol and pointed it at Joel.

“You will exit this aircraft right now. My job was to get you here and you’re here. Get off my bird.” He pointed it at Abby. “You too.”

“Okay okay. We’ll go.” Joel grabbed Abby’s hand and they trudged down the ramp.

He looked back at Ponzi. He motioned with

his pistol. Go on. And to make his point aimed it one more time at Joel. They stepped off the ramp onto the grass and walked from under the spinning rotors. As soon as he turned around, the engine began to rev up again. The prop blast blew sand into their eyes and they had to turn their heads as the helicopter lifted off again. They watched until the sound was gone and they could barely see the blinking red light from the helicopter as it headed out over the Gulf. He looked around.

The place was dark except for a few vapor lights along the fence he saw when they landed. As his eyes searched, he settled on the mound to his left. Everything else was flat but the mound rose from the ground with a concrete wall and a steel door in the front. A bunker. He had watched enough shows about world war two to know a bunker when he saw one. Or so he thought. As he was trying to figure out what it was, the door slowly opened.

“Abby?” He said.

"Yeah, I see it."

They both waited for whatever was going to come next. He was surprised by what he saw. A girl not much older than Abby, he thought, came through the door. She started walking towards them.

"Hi." She said.

"Hi." Joel said.

"You just get here? Of course you did. What am I saying? I heard the helicopter leave. I'm dumb." She said.

"Sorry?" Joel was confused.

"My fault. I'm Hannah." She held out her hand.

"Joel, Abby." He said.

"Welcome to the POD." Hannah said.

"The what?" Abby asked.

"The POD. Primary Operations Depot." Hannah said. "At least that what the sign says."

“Sign?” Joel asked.

“Yeah, inside. Everything is inside.” Hannah said. “Let me ask you something.”

“Okay.” Joel said.

“You been bit?” She asked.

“Why?” Joel asked.

“I’ve been bit. Cyrus has been bit. Figured that’s why we’re here. If you’ve been bit too, that kinda confirms it.” Hannah said.

“Cyrus?”

“Yeah, he was here when I got here. He doesn’t stay in the POD though.” Hannah pointed to the other end of the field they were in. Joel could make out the shape of a tent. “Claustrophobic or something. He doesn’t talk a lot either. Think he’s kind a slow in the head myself but he’s nice enough.”

Joel’s head was swimming. The fear was replaced with confusion.

"Anyway, there's plenty of stuff in the bunker. Food, weapons, clothes. Everything we need." Hannah said.

"Need for what?" Joel asked.

"To stay here." She said.

"Why?" Abby asked.

"I guess to keep us safe. I figure someone will come to collect us at some point but if they don't, man we got a lot of stuff to make do with." Hannah said. "You didn't answer my question. Have you been bit?"

"Yes but there's a lot of people who have been bit. Why bring us here?" Joel asked.

"Ah but I bet the dead ignore you, don't they?" Hannah said. "Yeah, me too. Well, they didn't at first obviously or I wouldn't have gotten bit. But after it happened I was, I guess, special. Cyrus too. They ignore you too don't they?"

"Yeah, they do."

“Both of you?” She turned Abby.

“Yeah, both of us.” She said.

“I knew it, I knew it. YOU HEAR THAT CYRUS? THEY’RE JUST LIKE US. I TOLD YOU.” She yelled. “He ignores me most of the time. Come on. Let me show you around the place.”

Joel looked at the strange girl. He looked at his daughter. Food, shelter, isolation. Maybe things were getting better. At least for them. He grabbed his backpack, Abby grabbed hers and they followed the strange girl into the bunker.

Part 2

What Remains

Keys and Locks

Tilly raised the binoculars and looked down the road. She could see the five of them heading towards the gate.

"They're coming." She said.

"Kind of early isn't it?" Raj asked as he raised himself from the chair on top of the bus.

"Maybe they're done." She said.

"Well, we haven't seen any deaduns in the street in a few days. Maybe you're right." He climbed down the ladder and waited by the gate. A few minutes later he heard the knock.

"Welcome back." Raj said as four of them came through.

"I'd like to talk to Kate and Bridger, do you know where they are?" Naomi asked. Raj nodded at the big man standing outside as he closed the gate. Cyrus nodded back.

"Bridger is probably at his house. You know which one it is?" Raj asked.

"Yes. And Kate?"

"I would guess she's at the big house helping Evelyn and Emma Grace get supper ready." Raj said.

"Back kind of early." Tilly leaned over the edge of the bus. "Running out of deaduns out there?"

"Just about." Joel said. "We got all the way to the edge of town before we found a decent sized group of them."

"Why do you call them that?" Abby asked. "Deaduns."

"Not sure. Ed started calling them that and it just kinda stuck. But not all of us call them that. Ham calls them stringers and Emma Grace and her crowd call them goners."

"We've just always called them infected." Abby said. "But I don't guess what you call them really matters."

"Guess not. We all know what they are." Tilly said.

"What's that?" Hannah asked.

"Forgotten." Tilly said. "By everyone they ever knew, everyone who ever knew them and everyone left alive. Just part of the landscape now."

"That's kinda sad." Abby said.

"This world is kind of a sad place now." Tilly said. "But maybe it won't be by the time this one grows up." She nodded at her own belly.

"Boy or girl?" Abby asked.

"I hope so." Tilly smiled. Abby smiled back.

Joel, Abby and Hannah started walking up the hill. Naomi paused and turned back to Raj.

“You spent time with Ramey? The one that was outside your walls?” She asked.

“Just briefly.”

“I’d like to get your assessment.” Naomi said. “When you have time.”

“There wasn’t much to assess. I don’t know what was happening to him physiologically so it would just be cursory.” Raj said.

“Maybe I can fill in the gaps of his physiological condition for you and you can maybe apply that to your observations.” Naomi said. “But like I said, when you have time.”

“We get off in a few hours.” Raj said.

“Hey if you wanna go do that I think I can handle sitting up here getting a suntan all by myself.” Tilly said.

“You sure?” Raj asked.

"Sure." Tilly said.

Raj agreed. He and Naomi started up the hill behind the others. They got to Raj's house and he led her back into the little exam room.

"So tell me, what were your initial impressions of Ramey?" Naomi asked.

"First let me ask you something. Charlie said that you and he visited Ramey and that he had begun to, I guess, be more like the deaduns."

"In a sense he was but he was cognizant of his actions. The infected aren't like that." Naomi said.

"What happened to him?" Raj asked.

"I did as he wished. He was in pain, unimaginable pain both physically and mentally."

"Charlie told me that was what he wanted but that's not what I meant. How did he get the way he was?" Raj asked.

"That's what I intend to find out." Naomi said.

"How can I help with that?"

"When you talked to him, I assume he told you the same story he told me. He was subjected to some type of experimental injection that resulted in his condition." She said.

"That's what I gathered although it was obvious when I talked to him it had been quite a traumatic experience." He said.

"Of course. How long ago was it you saw him?" She asked.

"Quite a while."

"What was his physical condition at that time?"

"Well he had a depressed heart rate and..."

"No, I'm sorry, I meant his appearance and his overall physical strength."

"He was in awful shape. Weak, sensitive to light but a heightened sense of smell according to his own account." He said.

"Weak?"

"Considerably. Why?"

"Just wondering. Have your people ever encountered any of the infected that were different?" Naomi asked.

"Different?" He asked.

"From the others. More capable than the shuffling husks we've been clearing out."

"Back when we were still out at the compound there was a wreck out on the road. Tilly, Evelyn, Charlie and I went to investigate. There was one that was different. It moved faster." He said.

"Did it look different?"

"Yeah, its skin had the consistency and color of dried meat. Leathery." Raj said.

"Anything else?"

"We killed it. But in the process part of its leg was cleaved open. The muscle underneath was inundated with a yellowish spider web like substance. I only got a brief look at it because there was a herd of deaduns closing in on us and we had to leave quickly." He said. "What is this all about?"

"You saw the webbing?"

"I did."

"That was the virus, Marionette. We called it OW1 but it's the same thing."

"From the comet?" Raj asked.

"You know about the connection?" Naomi asked.

"Just what your people told Scott. His story has made its way around. Is it true? You were bit years ago and the government hid it from everyone?" He asked.

"I was bit a long time before the outbreak. I guess I was part of those that helped hide it though so no need to go looking for anyone else to blame." She said.

"Sorry, wasn't trying to say it was anyone's fault but a little heads up, maybe."

"Would it have made any difference?" She asked.

"I guess we'll never know." His eyes narrowed.

"That's fair." Naomi said.

"Back to my question. What's this all about? All this stuff about Ramey and different deaduns?" He asked.

"There was a doctor. Her name was Sherrill but I only know that from a file. I've never met her. She was one of the people that were working on the problem." Naomi said. "That's who I think gave the injection to Ramey. He tried to remember her name. He couldn't but I know it was her."

"How?" He asked.

"She was assigned to Zone 3 and sent to South Springs Airfield. It was a civilian airport but it had originally been built during the sixties by the Army. There were underground facilities there and she started working on what every scientist they could round up was working on." She said.

"A cure? Vaccine?" Raj asked.

"Anything. Anything they could find that might stop all this from happening. Obviously it didn't work. But she was close." She said.

"How do you know?"

"We monitored communications. She found something. And when Scott told Noah about Ramey, it clicked that it might be her. And after I talked to him I'm even more convinced that it was." Naomi said.

"And you think you can find her? And do what?" Raj asked.

"I hope we can find her. But I don't know if it will make a difference. Ramey seemed to be more of a serious mistake than a step in the right direction."

"No argument there." Raj said. "But what does that have to do with your other question about if we had seen different deaduns?"

"Something Ramey said. He said he felt stronger, better after he had..."

"Ate someone?"

"Yes. Before it all went bad, there were a lot of theories within the circle of people who knew. Theories about what would happen if the virus went global. Most of it was wrong but the part that was right is that once someone is infected their body almost immediately begins to decay. That's why there is such obvious necrosis around the bite. Once they die the virus greatly slows the rate of decay but doesn't stop it. And from what we have encountered along the way that seems to be true. They do rot away, eventually. But there is something else happening. Something no one had anticipated but was confirmed, at least to me, by Ramey's admission."

"That he felt better? I don't understand." Raj said.

"Have you ever seen one attacking or eating an animal?"

"Ramey had taken bites of the horse. But he didn't kill it and eat it. He said he had an urge to do it but didn't know why. And he said it was really more of instinctual yearning than anything beneficial." Raj said.

"There's no real benefit, other than a slight satiation of hunger. It has to be from a human. That's what I believe."

"Why?"

"It's what the virus needs to evolve." She said.

"Evolve?"

"I think some of them are bigger and faster and maybe smarter because of it. The ones that have had ample supplies of living to feed on during the early stages of gestation." She said.

"I wasn't sure but I felt like the one we saw back then wasn't just different in appearance but was more aware, more dangerous, more evolved." Raj admitted. "I think I even used that word."

“You’re right. At least I think you are.” She said.

“What does that mean? For us?” He asked.

“I don’t know yet.” Naomi said. “But I think if I can find this doctor or even if I could just find out what she was working on, maybe it will tell us more about all of it.” She said.

“And you know where she is?” He asked.

“I know where she was. That’s our next step. That’s why I needed to talk to Kate and Bridger.”

“Why?”

“Because we’re finished with our obligation of cleaning the dead away from your walls and I need to get back to what we are supposed to be doing.” She said. “I’m going to ask them if we can borrow that big military truck down at the gate and go gather supplies from our old encampment. And then I’m going to start searching.”

For Now

The steam flashed from the pot on the stove. Emma Grace lifted the lid and the steam rolled out in a cloud.

“If you could set that colander in that other pot, I think the potatoes are ready.” Emma Grace said as she wrapped the towel around the handles.

Kate grabbed the colander from the counter and set it over the pot in the sink. The heat and steam boiled out into the room as Emma Grace poured everything into the other pot.

She poured the drained potatoes from the colander into the now empty pot and put the other one with the hot water in it back on the stove. She took the venison that Evelyn had finished dicing up and put it in the hot water.

"Now let that boil for just a little while." Emma Grace said.

They heard the squeal of the screen door. Kate stuck her head out of the kitchen.
"Need any help?" Bridger asked as he stepped inside.

"I think we've got everything under control." Kate said.

"Good, I can't really do anything in a kitchen but burn things anyway." Bridger said as he came into the room. Evelyn leaned against him as he wrapped his arms around her. "Is that some of the deer Vernon brought in the other day?"

"It is." She said. "But I've had your MRE breakfast, it's not that bad."

"Not that good either and that's just heating something up. Not really cooking." He glanced into the pot on the stove. "So not just beans and potatoes tonight?" He smiled.

The door squealed again.

"Hello?" They heard Naomi's voice.

"We're in here." Kate said.

Naomi came around the corner and stepped into the kitchen.

"Smells wonderful." She said. "Would it be possible for me to have a word with you?" She looked at Kate.

"Sure, go ahead." Kate said.

"We're finished with our agreement." She said. "Most of the infected have been removed from your walls."

"Removed?" Bridger asked. "To where?"

"They have been eradicated." She said bluntly.

"That was a lot of deaduns. Did you just leave them laying where they fell?" Bridger asked.

"Our standard procedure has always been to gather the infected that have been dispatched and dispose of the remains in a burn pit." Naomi said.

"And that's what you did?" Kate asked.

"It is."

"So you've been burning the corpses? Why haven't we seen the smoke?" Bridger asked.

"I don't know. Maybe you haven't been looking. If you don't believe me, I would be happy to take you out there and show you." Naomi said.

"I think you'll need to." Bridger said. "When would you like to go?"

"Is that really necessary?" Naomi asked.

"You've been given shelter and food in return for fixing the shit you and your people heaped on top of us. So yeah, it's necessary." Bridger said.

"Fine. But we are done. And after you've satisfied yourself that we aren't lying, I need to ask another favor." Naomi said.

"Another one? How many favors do you plan on asking for?" Bridger stepped around the table.

"I would like to borrow that deuce and a half you have sitting by the gate." Naomi said.

"You want our truck?"

"Just borrow it." Naomi said.

"Why?" Kate asked.

"We have a job to do. And we're ready to start doing it again. I'd like to borrow the truck so we can return to our compound and retrieve some supplies before we move on." Naomi said.

"So you're leaving?" Bridger said.

"Yes."

"Then yes, take it. As a matter of fact don't even worry about bringing it back. Just take it and go away." Bridger said.

"Hold on." Kate said.

"What?" Bridger said.

"I'll bring the truck back. I wouldn't deprive you of its use." Naomi said to Kate.

"That's not what concerns me." Kate said. "I don't want you or your people to go away."

"You're not planning on keeping them here?" Bridger asked.

"I have to agree with Bridger, I don't think you can keep us here." Naomi said.

"Oh, we can do whatever the hell we want, just like you people did with her son." Bridger said. "We can keep you here, we can march you out the gates and blow your brains out if we want to. Nothing you can do to stop it."

"Bridger. That's enough." Kate said. "Naomi, you can use the truck. But we will send some of our people with you."

"Why?"

"Because I said so. Look, I don't know what your job is or what you are planning to do but you've made it clear that there is something out there that may offer us another chance." Kate said. "I'm not just going to let go of that."

"So you intend to keep us against our will?" Naomi asked.

"No, but I intend on keeping you under close supervision." Kate said. "I don't want that to be confrontational. You said you were doing this job so you could help people, we're people. And since we have given you sanctuary here, I think you at least owe us that courtesy."

"But I don't know if we'll find anything. Caleb may have been right. This might be nothing." Naomi said. "I don't want you to be disappointed. There may not be anything left to find."

"Well, we'll figure that out together. I won't be disappointed. You have to have expectations to be disappointed. I don't expect anything except that you trust us. Wasn't that the whole point of what Noah did? He said trust was built over yours and Scott's lives." Kate said.

“He did.” She lowered her head slightly. “You’re right. We’ll want to head to our old compound tomorrow morning if that’s possible and I welcome whoever you want to send with us.” Naomi looked at Bridger.

“Oh, you know I’m going. I’m not letting you out of my sight unless I know it will be the last time I see you.” Bridger said.

“Very well, tomorrow morning then.” Naomi said. She turned and headed back out the door. They heard the screen door squeal. Kate turned to Bridger.

“What the hell was that?” She asked.

“Nothing.” He said.

“Bullshit. Tell me now.” Kate’s voice hardened.

“I don’t trust them Kate. That one right there is chasing something besides what she says she is chasing.” Bridger said.

“What’s that?”

"Redemption. If all her story is true, she was part of hiding all this. She's wrapped up in guilt and that makes her dangerous." Bridger said.

"Well, good thing you're going to be the one keeping an eye on her." Kate said.

"I want Jahda, Devin and Charlie to go too." Bridger said.

"Why Devin?" Emma Grace asked.

"Because I trust him to keep his cool. Jahda and Charlie too." Bridger said.

"Why is that important?" Emma Grace asked.

"Just in case I can't." Bridger said.

Naomi walked down the sidewalk and paused when she got to the street. She looked to her left and saw a man with a limp walking towards her. She couldn't remember his name.

"Good evening." The man said.

“Good evening uh…” Naomi said.

“Cameron.”

“Yes, Cameron.” Naomi said.

“Care to join me on my stroll?” Cameron asked.

“Sorry?”

“I am exercising this bum ankle. It has healed wonderfully thanks to the efforts of Dr. Raj but it does require a bit a loosening up on occasion.” He said.

“I’m surprised.” Naomi said.

“Well, when you have had as many birthdays as I have had things don’t heal up quite as efficiently. Alas, the failure to mark the occasions on the calendar seems to be quite irrelevant to the actual passage of time.” He said.

“I’m sure. But I’m surprised that you would want my company. It seems most of your companions have come to the conclusion I am a company they would rather not keep unless they have to.” She said.

"What do you mean?" He asked as they started down the middle of the street.

"Well Bridger made it clear he doesn't trust me and has no intention of wanting to." She said. "Kate has reserved judgment though, at least until she can determine if we can be of any particular use."

"And you find that disconcerting?" He asked.

"Wouldn't you?" She asked.

"When I first met these people, I found myself in a very similar position as you find yourself in now." He said.

"How so?" She asked.

"I wasn't with this group in the beginning. I was alone. But I had the great fortune of an unexpected visit by Kate's late husband as the world unwound. That random connection led me to this group shortly after her husband was lost. He made an impression on me that I wasn't even aware of at the time. After I accidentally burnt my former abode to ashes I became a wanderer. I met our resident equine and she and I found these people. But before I found them, I found where they had been. It was just a wide spot on an old dirt road. They had started with nothing. But they managed to end up with an entire town surrounded by an exceptional barricade against the dead."

"How?"

"Guile and determination."

"And guns?"

"Not entirely. There was an altercation, as I was told, in the early days between Tilly and some ne'er-do-well. They ended up absconding his domicile after his untimely but intentional demise."

"They killed him?"

"Tilly reacted at his attempt to procure her for his own amusement with determined and irrevocable resolve." Cameron said.

"That is a hell of a turn of a phrase." Naomi smiled. "But I'm not judging. Everyone has done things to survive." Naomi said.

"Including welcoming people into their fold in spite of the conditions throughout the world almost insisting that they don't." Cameron said. "Now make no mistake, they are not to be trifled with but they are not inherently nor deliberately threatening. Since I have been fortunate to count myself among their ranks, I have seen what I truly believe to be the best of humanity. They have suffered but in their suffering they have found strength."

"I'm sure. I had just hoped they would welcome us instead of suspecting us." Naomi said.

"They have welcomed you. But they will be suspicious until they aren't." Cameron said.

"When will that be?" Naomi sighed.

"When Tilly encountered and dispatched the ne'er-do-well I previously mentioned he was not alone. He had an accomplice. A partner." Cameron said.

"What happened to him?"

"You see that man over there sitting on the couch that has been relocated to the front porch?" Cameron said.

"The guy that looks like he's stoned all the time?"

"Ha, yes. That's Ed. He was the partner. And yet here he sits." Cameron said. "Under the circumstances of their meeting he truly has no reason to be alive. They could have dispatched him and left him to become another lost story buried in the mud and no one would have ever missed him. But they didn't. Not because he has anything to offer or anything of worth, but because they do."

"What's that?"

"Simple compassion and a providence given appreciation of life. And even though they may now seem to be antagonistic towards you, I promise they are only that way because they have to be." Cameron said. "They are searching for a way to accept you and they will do so until they have satisfied for themselves that you are worth accepting."

"We are." Naomi said.

"I take you at your word. But words are cheap commodities in these days." Cameron said.

"Well maybe tomorrow we'll start getting past words. It seems we are going to be working together. Even if it is as the watchers and the watched." Naomi said.

Moving

The next morning, as the sun began to brighten the eastern sky and the clouds began slowly spreading apart, Kate stepped onto the porch. Between the clumps of grass and weeds that now spread through the cracks of the road, the asphalt underneath sparkled in the wet left over from the night's showers. Scott stood in the yard watching the two people walk down the street towards the house.

"Good morning Scott." Abby said.

"Good morning Abby, you too Joel." He nodded.

"Is your mother around?" Joel asked.

"Right up there." Scott pointed to the figure lingering under the shadow of the porch.

Joel and Abby walked down the walk towards the porch. Scott followed.

"Good morning Kate." Joel said. "I know we haven't really gotten to talk much but I was wondering if you could do me a favor."

"Depends on what you have in mind but I'll try." Kate said as she met them at the top of the steps.

"Nothing all that difficult. I would just like for you to keep an eye on Abby for me." Joel said.

"Dad thinks I need a baby sitter. I don't." Abby protested.

"I'm not trying to get a baby sitter. I just want to know that you're going to be okay." He said.

"I can go with you." Abby said.

"No, not an option." He said.

"It's cool. You can help me split wood for the

stove." Scott said.

"See, you have a job now." Joel said.

"Fine." Abby said.

"Come on." Scott said. They walked around the other side of the house where the wood was stacked. Joel and Kate watched them go.

"Why isn't it an option? She's one of you right? Immune?" Kate asked.

"She is. But we're going back to our compound. I don't know if Caleb left anyone behind to guard it or not. I'd rather not take the risk of putting her in a situation we may not be prepared for." Joel said.

"You think they would be violent?" Kate asked.

"I don't know. But I made a promise a long time ago I would do everything I could to keep her safe." Joel said.

"But these people you are afraid of were your friends, right?" Kate said.

“They were. And they may still be, but I’m not sure. And that means I won’t take the risk.” Joel said.

“If they’re so dangerous why were you with them in the first place.” Kate asked.

“In the beginning we didn’t have a choice. They were the only option. And that was fine. Everything was good. I thought I had lost her when this first began. I was given a second chance with our group. Hannah and Cyrus were the first two we met that were like us. I trust them more than anyone now. When they said it was time to leave, I didn’t even ask why.” Joel said.

“But the others?” Kate asked.

“Good people. I guess. But there were issues. I didn’t need Hannah or Cyrus to tell me that. You could feel the tension as time went on.”

“Tension over what?” Kate asked.

“Direction. Leadership. Purpose. All the things that bring empires down.”

“That’s what you thought you had? An empire?” Kate raised her eyebrow.

“No, just making a comparison.” Joel said. “The infighting was almost every day by the time your son showed up.”

“He didn’t show up. Your people took him.” Kate said as she felt a surprising tinge of anger rise up.

“I’m sorry. Cyrus was just trying to make sure he and the girl…”

“Ham.” Kate interjected.
“He and Ham were safe. He found them alone in the woods. He was just trying to protect them.” Joel said.

“And now you want me to return the favor or something?” Kate asked.

“Listen, I don’t mean to upset you. But I am going to do whatever I have to do to make sure she is safe.” Joel said.

“I’m sorry. I’m not upset. Of course we’ll watch

her. I didn't mean to be so...well you know." Kate said.

"It's okay. Thank you." Joel turned to walk away.

"It's just that I spent a week worrying if I had failed to keep Scott safe. Worrying if I was ever going to see him again. It tore me apart. Some of the pieces are still trying to fit back into place." Kate said.

Joel paused and looked back. He smiled.

"Fair enough." He turned towards the street. She watched him as he walked away.

Jennifer stood at the open gate. The truck was parked beside the bus. She watched Josh and Lori as they helped the others climb into the back.

"Got everything you need?" Bridger asked as Jahda and Devin climbed into the back of the truck with Charlie, Joel and Hannah.

“Yeah, we’re ready.” Jahda said. “What do you expect out there?”

“I don’t know. It should be simple. But she’s not sure if some of their group is still there or not.” Bridger said.

“You got a plan if they are?” Devin asked.

“Plan? You two are my plan.” Bridger said. “I’ve seen both of you get into and out of all kinds of shit. I figure you’ll just keep doing what you been doing.” He smiled.

“We like running.” Devin said.

“Best plan I’ve heard in a month.” Bridger slapped the back of the tailgate as he latched it in place. Naomi came around the side of the truck. “Ready?” She asked.

“Why not.” Bridger said. “You drive. You know the way right?”

“I know the way.” She said.

“Good. First though, I want you to take me to your

burn pit. Trust but verify and all that." He said.

"Sure. Let's go." She said. They climbed into the cab of the truck.

Bridger watched as she flipped the switch on and hit the start button.

"You've driven a deuce before?" He raised his voice over the engine noise.

"Yeah, I love these old fuckers." She smiled.

"Well, let's go then." He sat back.

Jennifer closed the gate behind them and climbed the ladder to the top of the bus.

The truck rolled down the street for about a quarter mile and stopped.

"What are we stopping for?" Bridger asked.

"Cyrus." Naomi said. "He's joining us."

Bridger watched as the big man that stays outside their gates appeared at the door of the house they had stopped in front of.

"He lives here?"

"He lives out here." Naomi said. "He feels safer among the infected than among the living."

"Why?"

"He never really talks about it but I know it has a lot more to do with things that happened to him before." Naomi said.

"How so?"

"Let's just say that his world went to shit a long time before it did for the rest of us." She said.

Bridger watched in the side mirror as Cyrus climbed in the back of the truck with the rest of them. They started down the road again.

The flicker of sunlight through the trees jostled Bridger from his daydream. The truck's monotonous drone and the smell of diesel had taken him back to a different time. He looked around and realized they were getting close to the co-op. She slowed and they took the little side road that ran parallel to the parking lot. They drove between the two fields and Bridger began to smell spent gasoline and something else. She didn't need to point it out to him when they pulled to a stop. He got out and slung his rifle over his shoulder.

There was a dirt turnout that the last farmer that planted these fields probably used to park his tractor in between plowing and sewing. The dirt was burnt. He could see dozens of skulls among the mixture of ash and bone. He walked closer. Some were still smoldering slightly and the wisps of smoke settled over the piles like fog clinging to the moist ground. The smell was sickeningly sweet.

"Satisfied?" Naomi asked as she walked up beside him.

"Yeah." He said.

He turned and looked at the others standing in the bed of the truck looking over the blackened landscape in front of them. Jahda nodded her head and sat back down. The others followed her lead.

"Let's go." Bridger said as he turned and climbed back in the cab.

Abby sat down beside the tree and took a drink from the water bottle. She wiped the rim and stuck the bottle out towards Scott.

"Want some?" She asked.

He put the axe down and wiped his forehead with his sleeve.

"Sure." He took the bottle and drank.

"I wish we had been here the whole time." She said. "It's nice."

"We didn't start here." He said.

"Where did you come from?" She asked.

"South Springs." He said.

"Where's that?" She asked.

"Seems like a long ways away. But I guess it's really only about a hundred miles, probably less." He said.

"Do you want to go back?" She asked.

"I don't know, maybe. Where are you from?"

"Atlanta." She said. "It doesn't even seem like a real place now. Like a memory of a dream or something."

"That's where it happened? Your bite?" Scott asked.

"Yeah." She sighed.

"Sorry, I don't mean to upset you. Hannah told me kind of what happened." He said.

"It's okay. I just don't like talking about it." She said.

"I understand. I don't talk about what happened to my dad either." He said.

“Do you want too?” She asked.

“I don’t know. Sometimes. I miss him. I try to remember him. His voice. Sometimes when it’s really quiet, I can almost hear it. But then it’s gone.” He said.

“What was he like?”

“He was a dad. He was goofy and clumsy. He was hard at times but he tried to be a friend when Josh and me needed it. I really never knew what he was like when he was in the army. I was just a baby when he got out. Mom doesn’t really talk about it but I know he had bad dreams and stuff. I remember when I was maybe three or four waking up in the middle of the night to pee. I could hear him crying in the living room. He was watching some war movie and crying like a baby. It scared me.” He said.

“Scared you?”

“Yeah, I didn’t think he cried. I thought he was sick or something. He was I guess but I didn’t know how."

"What do you mean?"

"He had nightmares from the things he had to do in the army. Mom told me once that he had to keep a lot of stuff inside because no one really understood. He went to the VA once a month to talk to people who did." He said.

"Did it help?" She asked.

"Yeah. I guess it did. When I was little, he used to yell a lot. But by the time I was ten or twelve I almost never heard him raise his voice. Funny the things you remember." He smiled.

"My mom was pretty strict. But she didn't yell. She just grounded me." Abby said.

"Grounded you? For what?" He asked.

"Stupid stuff. Bad grades mostly." She said. "My first year of middle school was pretty hard. I kind of started hanging out with this girl that was really mature." Abby held her hands out in front of her chest. “Know what I mean?”

“Yeah.” He smiled sheepishly.

“Well she kept me in trouble. I skipped class a few times and got caught smoking at school.” Abby said. “Mom freaked.”

“What did she do?”

“Well, I don’t think I talked to Gina, that was the girls name, for a year. Mom called the school and made them change my schedule so we barely crossed paths. She wouldn’t let me use my phone for like six months.” She said.

“That’s harsh.” He said.

“That’s what I said.” Abby smiled. “But now I’d give almost anything to see that look on her face when she’s really pissed. I’d give almost anything to see her at all.”

“Me too.”
“You’d like to see my mom?” She smiled.

“No, my dad.” He looked at her. “You knew what I

meant."

"Yeah. And yeah." She stood. "We're a lot alike ain't we? Half orphans."

"Half orphans. I like that." He said. "I think we have enough for a while." He looked over the pile of split wood. "You wanna help me stack it?"

"Can't I just sit here and watch you do it? I'd rather not get all dirty." She said as she stood.

He looked at her. Her face was smeared in sweat and dirt and her hands were as blistered as his from swinging the axe. Her clothes were covered in dirt with wood chips clinging to the sweat that had soaked through.

"Are you serious?" He asked.

She tilted her head and put her hands on her hips.

"You're not. Okay, I get it." Scott smiled. "Let's get this finished up."

"And then?" She asked as she started grabbing

pieces of wood.

“And then we eat.” He said.

“I really do like this place. I mean it.” She said.

“You think you wanna stay?” He asked as he stacked the wood on the pile.

“I’d like to but it’s up to my dad.” She said.

“He won’t let you?” He asked.

“It’s not that. I’m not going to leave him. Wherever he goes, I go. We have to stay together. That’s what my mom wanted.” She said.

“Maybe he’ll want to stay too.” Scott said.

The Hour Grows Late

Bridger leaned forward in his seat. The road had almost disappeared completely as they drove between the trees.

“You sure you know the way?” He asked.

“We’re here.” She smiled.

She stopped the truck. He could see the gate swung open and the fence disappearing into the trees on either side of the road.

“Did they leave the gate open?” Bridger asked as they all climbed out of the truck.

“It wasn’t open the last time I was here.” Cyrus said.

“When was that?” Jahda asked.

“A week ago.” He said.

“How many times have you been here since they left Cyrus?” Naomi asked.

“Three.” Cyrus said. “I came the day you asked me to. I watched them leave. I came back two days later to make sure they had gone.”

“And the third time?” Bridger asked.

“I came back last week to see if any of them had come back.” Cyrus said.

“Why?”

“I miss them. Some of them.” Cyrus said. “They were my friends.”

“We’re your friends Cyrus.” Hannah said.

"I know." He nodded his head. "Always. But they were too."

"Maybe we'll see them again." Joel said.

"I hope so." Cyrus said.

"Well, now that we have that out of the way, who opened the gate?" Bridger asked.

"Maybe some of them came back." Cyrus said. Bridger looked at Naomi. She shrugged.

"You think that's possible?" Bridger asked Naomi.

"Maybe." She said.

"If they did, how would they react to seeing you?" Jahda asked.

"I'm not sure." She said.

"How much further down this road until we get to the trailers?" Bridger asked. "Scott said y'all had lots of trailers."

"Half a mile. This was the back gate. This pine thicket runs for another quarter mile and then everything opens up." Naomi said.

"If it is your people would they fire on us? Would they fire on someone they didn't know just showing up?" Bridger asked.

"I don't know. Before this happened, before Noah died, I could have told you no, they wouldn't. But I don't know now." Naomi said.

"Well, we'll just have to take a chance. Okay, here's what we're going to do." Bridger started.

Naomi stopped the truck just as the top of the first trailer came into view. She waited a few seconds and laid down on the horn. The sound ripped through the air. She counted ten and laid down on it again. She opened the door and jumped out.

She ran into the woods and ducked down one tree over from the one Bridger sat behind.

"Now what?" She whispered.

"We wait." He said. "It won't take long if someone is in there."

Ten minutes later Bridger heard a motorcycle coming down the crushed gravel road from the direction of the trailers. The bike stopped beside the truck and the two people on it got off. He looked at Jahda and held up two fingers. He pointed at her, held his palm towards her and then towards him. 'Wait until I go then follow me.'

She held her ground. He turned to Naomi.

"You see them?" He whispered.

"Yeah." She said.

"You recognize them?"

"No. I don't know who they are." She whispered back.

"Okay. Stay here." He said.

He turned his head towards Jahda. He put

his palm towards her again and gave her a thumbs up. He slipped around the tree and shouldered his rifle. Jahda fell in behind him with her pistol in hand and they started towards the truck that was a few dozen yards through the trees. The two people were climbing up on the running boards and looking inside. As Bridger and Jahda cleared the tree line, he gave a short whistle.

"Hey guys. Can I help you?" He said as he shouldered his rifle.

The two people, a man and a woman turned at the sound of his voice. Both of them stuck their hands in the air. Jahda held her pistol on them.

"Hey, hey no reason to do that." The man said.

"That's our truck." Bridger said.

"Oh, I didn't know. I just heard the horn blow and came to see what was going on." The man said.

"Came from where?" Bridger asked.

"Down there." The man nodded towards the

trailers.

“What’s down there?” Bridger asked.

“Our place.” The woman said.

“That’s not your place. Lie one more time.” Bridger said as he flipped the safety off.

“Okay, okay. It’s not really our place. We just found it.” The man said.

“What makes you think it was lost?”

“Sorry?”

“You’re trespassing.” Bridger said. “How many more of you are down there?”

“No one. It’s just us.” The woman said.

“Where did you come from?” Jahda asked.

“Now look, we ain’t trespassing. There ain’t no sign.” The man said.

“The gate was locked.” Bridger said.
“Yeah well a lot of gates got left locked. How was

we to know this one was any different?" The man asked. "Look buddy, we didn't know this was your place."

"Well now you do." Bridger said.

"That's a lot of stuff down there for just the two of you." The woman said.

"You're half right." Bridger said. "That is a lot of stuff down there, but it's not just the two of us." Bridger said.

"How many are you?" The man asked.

"Enough to need all that stuff down there." Bridger said. "How many of you are there?"

"Just us two." The woman said.

"Well we're looking for new recruits all the time. You wanna join us?" Bridger asked. Jahda shot him a look. He ignored it.

"No, no. Appreciate the offer though." The man said. "That wasn't a join us or die offer was it?"
"If it was?" Bridger asked.

"Was it?" The man asked.

"No, but it was a join us or I better never see your ass again offer." Bridger said.

"That won't be any problem at all." The man said. "So we can go now?"

"One more question." Bridger said. "What's your name?"

"Well before all this happened I was someone else." The man said. "I guess we all were, huh?"

"I'm interested in who you are now." Bridger said.

"Now, I'm just another nobody. But folks have taken to calling me Little John. Not sure why but hey, gotta call me something I guess." Little John said.

"And you?" He asked the woman.

"Trish." She said.

"Do you have a name?" Little John asked.

"You don't need to know it." Bridger said.

"Then why do you need to know ours?" Little John asked.

"In case you come back, I need something to write on your tombstone." Bridger said. "Get on your bike, go away. Now."

The two looked at them for another few seconds. They climbed onto the motorcycle and drove away. The others came out from behind the trees and joined Bridger and Jahda beside the truck.

"You didn't know them?" Jahda asked.

"No, never seen them before." Naomi said.

"Well, we need to get in here and get out as quick as we can." Bridger said.

"You think they'll come back?" Hannah asked. "It's just the two of them."

"They're part of a group." Bridger said. "And they'll be back."

"How do you know they're part of a group?" Joel

asked.

“How much stuff is in those trailers down there?” Bridger asked.

“Lots. Everything. Food, clothing, shelter, weapons. You name it there’s a bit of anything needed to help rebuild from natural disaster and it was bulked up ahead of this with anything else they thought would be useful.” Naomi said.

“And how many places like this are out there?” Bridger asked.

“Seventeen sites spread out all over the country. Or there were.” Naomi said.

“How many within a hundred miles of here?” He asked.

“Just this one.” She said.

“Well they were going through that stuff down there.” Bridger said. “What’s down there is more precious than gold ever was. If it were just the two of them, they would have jumped at the chance to join in on that. But they turned me down when I offered without any hesitation. No, they're part of a bigger group. And they'll be back. We need to get what we can get and then get home before they get back with their friends."

"You think they're dangerous?" Joel asked.

"If what you say is down there is there, yeah. This new world has a made people desperate and people are always dangerous when they're desperate." Bridger said. "Ain't much left of the old world except people and people ain't changed one damned bit. And I would just as soon not have to deal with them."

The motorcycle rolled to a stop under an overhanging oak. He waited for the woman to get off before he put the kickstand down. He threw his leg over the seat and leaned against the bike as he lit a cigarette and listened to the wind blow. The woman came from the other side of the tree zipping her pants.

“So?” She asked.

“So what?”

“So what do you think?”

“Well our new friends weren’t lying about it being there. But they did lie when they said no one else knew about it.” He blew the smoke through his nose as he talked.

“Maybe they didn’t know.” She said.

“Maybe. But she’s already pissed the ones we laid out for her never stood back up. When she finds out the ones we left alive were lying to us, she’ll lose it. And that could get all of us laid out.” He said.

“So what do we do?” She asked.

“I think we’ll bring some of her children back over here. Then we’ll see just how tough that asshole is.” He said.

“You think she’ll do that? Bring the children?” She asked.

“Well, it’s going to take some smooth talking but yeah, she will.” He smiled.

“What about that lying asshole that sent us here?” She asked.

“I don’t know. She’ll probably feed him to the beast. I would. If I work it right, she may end up thanking me for bringing them to her anyway.” He said.

“But they ain’t walking. She ain’t going to thank you for that.” She said as she climbed back on the motorcycle.

He stubbed the cigarette out on the gravel in the road. He looked back towards where they had just come from. He stepped over the seat and hit the starter button on the bike. It fired up.

“Yeah, but she’ll be happy when I tell her we found some replacements.” He smiled as he eased off the clutch. The back tire spun a little gravel as he gripped the throttle. The bike straightened up and he steered it into the afternoon sun.

MUSIC FOR WHAT REMAINS

Katie Herzig
Ben Nichols
John Moreland
Lyle Lovett
Young Summer
The Dead Tongues
Lee DeWyze
Flatland Cavalry
The Be Good Tonyas
Townes Van Zandt
Leo
Jamie N Commons
The Belleville Outfit
The Dirty River Boys
Andrea von Kampen
Jose' Gonzalez
Amy Stroup
Passenger
John Fullbright
Mandolin Orange
The Honey Dewdrops
Dead Horses
Parker Milsap
Matthew Perryman Jones
The Greencards
Patty Griffin
Thieving Birds
Rock Plaza Central
Crooked Still

Coming Soon

Wasteland

Book 14

The Marionette Zombie Series

By

SB Poe

www.ingramcontent.com/pod-product-compliance
Ingram Content Group UK Ltd.
Pitfield, Milton Keynes, MK11 3LW, UK
UKHW040022200726
13854UKWH00001B/307

9 798507 100804